ONE LAST SHOT

ONE LAST SHOT

STEPHEN ANTHONY BROTHERTON

The Book Guild Ltd

First published in Great Britain in 2020 by
The Book Guild Ltd
9 Priory Business Park
Wistow Road, Kibworth
Leicestershire, LE8 0RX
Freephone: 0800 999 2982
www.bookguild.co.uk
Email: info@bookguild.co.uk
Twitter: @bookguild

Typeset in Minion Pro

Printed and bound in Great Britain by CPI Group (UK) Ltd, Croydon, CR0 4YY

ISBN 978 1913208 509

British Library Cataloguing in Publication Data.
A catalogue record for this book is available from the British Library.

FSC
MIX
Paper from
responsible sources
FSC® C013604
www.fsc.org

John Brotherton: *'I never really knew you, Dad,*
but I've missed you always.'

Other Books by Stephen Anthony Brotherton:

Another Shot (2017)
An Extra Shot (2019)

I was sitting on a bench in the gardens of the Hotel Rushmore, sipping my peppermint tea and thinking about the thirty-five years ago clinic with its paper sheets, women's magazines, omnipresent antiseptic, pain, vomit and black-hole nothingness. I placed my hand on my stomach and sighed. 'Oh, Freddie,' I said.

The French doors to the hotel restaurant opened and Amy walked out, closed the door behind her and strode across the lawn. She sat down next to me and squeezed my knee. 'You okay?' she said.

I nodded, my hand still on my stomach.

'Dan's booked the flights, Mum. We leave the end of the week. If that's what you still want.'

'It's been two days, Amy. He's not going to phone.'

'Dan thinks you should call him.'

'You've discussed this with Dan?'

'He is your son-in-law. He cares about you.'

'I did wonder about calling Jack,' I said. 'But it feels like I'm a stalker. And if Freddie's made his decision…'

'Didn't all this start with missed phone-calls? Don't let pride get in the way.'

'You're right,' I said, reaching into my bag and pulling out my Samsung phone. 'Jack must have spoken to him.'

'I'll get us some more tea,' said Amy, picking up my cup and saucer from the lawn. She stood up and walked off towards the hotel.

I scrolled down my contacts list and tapped on Jack's name.

*

We had a full view of the car park through the glass doors of the hotel reception area. Amy was picking at her fingernails. It was

1

something she did when she was concentrating. I'd spent most of her childhood trying to stop her, but that just made her anxious. I was churning over the possibilities of what might have happened. Jack had sounded serious, but he didn't want to give me the details over the phone. 'I wonder why Jack didn't call me earlier,' I said.

'Perhaps he felt a bit awkward,' said Amy.

'Or perhaps something's happened today.'

'That would be huge coincidence, Mum.'

'He's here,' I said, nodding towards the car park.

Jack's Mini was reversing into one of the visitor bays.

*

Amy linked her arm in mine and we walked out of the reception and onto the hotel patio. Jack ran up the concrete steps and hugged me. 'This is my daughter, Amy,' I said.

'Hi,' said Jack, shaking her hand.

'Is Freddie okay?' I said.

'Let's go and sit in the garden,' said Amy.

We reached the bench and sat down. Amy had filled the short walk across the lawn with small talk, asking Jack if he'd found the hotel okay, saying how much she loved his car. Jack had kept his eyes on the grass, nodding occasionally, muttering monosyllabic answers, all of which raised my anxiety. 'Isn't this garden lovely?' said Amy.

'What's happened to Freddie, Jack?' I said.

'He's okay,' he said. 'But he took your news pretty badly.'

'It wasn't an easy thing for Mum to tell him,' said Amy. 'I told her not to. It's nothing to do with him really. After what he…'

'Tell me what's happened,' I said.

'You know what he's like,' said Jack, tears welling in his eyes. 'He blames himself for everything.'

'You're a good friend,' I said, squeezing his hand. 'You always have been.'

He returned my squeeze and met my eyes. 'He fell in love with you the moment he saw you, Jo-Jo. You do know that, don't you?'

'Yes,' I said. 'And I've never stopped loving him. Tell me what's happened.'

'He's okay.'

'You've said that already.'

He looked at the grass again.

'She needs to know,' said Amy.

*

An hour later, Jack had left us sitting on the bench. I was trying to clear my head, create a distraction by thinking about something else. Lawrence Coulson's Midnight Chimes picture, a moonlit sky, a white circle of light, clouded over and sucking you into the canvas through different hues of blue into darkness, moonbeams reflecting off a lake, shadows of a hilly landscape, a brick tower with a pinprick of yellow electric light escaping from its attic. I tried to focus on the light, let it fill the void in my head, let everything else blur out of existence. I wondered what the room looked like inside, a barred window, limestone walls covered in lichenous fungi...

'I need to see him,' I said.

'Is that a good idea? I know he wants to see you, but Jack said he's still in a bad way.'

'I can't just walk away from him.'

'This isn't your fault, Mum. None of this is your fault. You've just told him something you felt he had a right to know. There must be something wrong with him.'

'He's always been vulnerable,' I said.

'And you haven't seen him for over thirty years. You don't owe him anything.'

'I need to make sure he's alright.'

'Okay,' she said. 'But I'm coming with you.'

One, two, three, four. I moved the front door handle up and down. It's locked. No it isn't. One more time. One, two, three, four. I can feel Mo, my neighbour, watching me through her grey net curtains. One, two, three, four. Check it again. I heard a car turn into the street and drive past the house. I turned to walk away from the door. It's still open. No it isn't. Yes it is. I turned back. One, two, three, four. 'Freddie.' An arm dropped around my shoulder. 'Come on, Freddie. Let's go back to mine.' I looked at him, tears dripping off my face, snot bunging up my nose.

'I can't lock the door, Jack. The bloody thing won't lock.'

'Leave it,' he said, prising my hand off the handle.

I looked at him again. 'I should have been there,' I said.

'Come on,' he said, hugging me to him and walking me to the car.

*

The car park of the boat yard take-out point in Ironbridge was empty and a mid-afternoon tarpaulin of hush had dropped over the day's activities. We were going to sit in our usual thinking place on the concrete steps leading into the River Severn, but the overnight rain had submerged four of the six steps and Jack led me to the top of the grassy embankment. We sat down on a bench and stared out at the fast-flowing current. A raft of ducks, two adults and four ducklings, sped past us, carried along at break-neck speed, casting ripples of motion across the surface of the water, the lead duck honking loudly out of exhilaration or possibly fear. Neither of us had said a word during the ten-minute car journey. 'You okay?' said Jack, finally breaking the silence.

'I can't believe it,' I said.

'Believe what? You still haven't told me what's happened.'

I looked at him. 'I thought Jo-Jo had called you. What made you come round?'

'Your neighbour phoned me. You'd been on that doorstep for half an hour. What's wrong, Freddie?'

I regurgitated the three-decades-old news. It felt like someone else was telling the story, like I was eavesdropping the conversation, the emptiness in my stomach growing by the second as though some vital organ was being sucked out of me. I felt Jack's hand on my leg. 'I should have been there,' I said.

'How could you have been? You didn't even know.'

'But I shouldn't have walked away in the first place.'

'You can't do anything about that now. You've got to deal with the present. Leave the past where it belongs.'

'But we could have had a baby. That would have made all the difference.'

'And it could just as easily have pulled you apart. You don't know how it would have worked out.'

I looked at the river. The ducks had disappeared, but further along the bank a man was screwing together two halves of a fishing rod. He reached into a wicker basket and fetched out a pencil case-size wooden box. It looked like it was made out of rosewood and, I guessed, contained his bait. He made his selection, fixed a shimmering blue fly to the end of the line and cast off into the water. The line landed with a plop, bobbed up and down for a few seconds before he reeled it back in and cast off again. It re-landed in pretty much the same spot, but this time he left it, secured the rod into a bank stick and sat down on a green canvas picnic chair. 'Why do fisherman do that?' I said.

'What?' said Jack.

'Cast their line a couple of times before they're happy. It always seems to land in the same place.'

He shrugged. 'I guess they know what they're doing,' he said.

The fisherman reached into the wicker basket again and fetched out a red thermos flask. He unscrewed the lid, filled up a plastic cup, held it against his face cheek for a few seconds before blowing on the contents and taking a sip. He stared at the bobbing float, waiting for a sign that he'd tempted something to take a bite. 'Bob does that,' I said. 'Holds his cup against his face.'

'Does he?'

'Whenever he takes a drink. It must be a comfort thing. Haven't you noticed?'

He looked at the fisherman. 'You need to talk to her, Freddie.'

'I can't,' I said.

'She did what she thought was right. You can't blame her for that.'

'I don't blame her. I blame me.'

He stood up and brushed the step dust off the back of his jeans. 'Let's go for a walk,' he said.

We walked side by side through the park, past the craft centre and onto the narrow path of the high street, the River Severn on our right-hand side as we headed up the hill towards the bridge. We stopped at a wooden bench to read the inscription on the seat – *'In loving memory of Terry. I hope you enjoy the view as much as he did.'*

'Not our Terry,' said Jack. 'Nice gesture though. We should talk to Bob about getting something done.' A man and a woman came towards us, walking a black labradoodle. Jack stepped into the road to let them by, the dog looked up at him, the expression on his face saying, 'I should think so too,' as he plodded past. There was no-one else around, which was unusual for such a nice day in August. I looked at my watch. 'It's only seven thirty,' I said.

'You've probably been up for hours. Did you get any sleep last night?'

'Not much. I kept playing it over and over in my head.'

'I know it's hard, Freddie, but it was a long time ago. You got on well in Devon, didn't you?'

'The best.'

'There you are then.'

We walked past the café in the square, where we'd stop sometimes and have a cafetière of Jamaican Blue coffee and a slice of homemade Victoria Sandwich. We stopped on the bridge and stood peering down through the railings at the river. 'I wonder how many lovers have stood here,' I said.

'Thousands, I should think,' said Jack. 'It's two hundred years old.'

'And I couldn't wait for three. That's all she was asking, time to do her degree, but I chose to walk away from her and the baby.'

'You didn't know about the baby. You've got to stop punishing yourself for something you can't change, enjoy the fact you've got a second chance.'

'Maybe,' I said. 'But it all feels like such a waste.'

'Then don't waste any more time. Call her.'

Freddie's Dream

'Wake up.'

The voice is soothing. I want to obey, but my eyelids feel stitched shut. I lift my right arm and touch my face. My skin feels cold. 'Wake up.'

'Who are you?'

I'm surprised to hear my own voice. I'd made the words sound demanding. 'Be careful,' I tell myself. 'At least until you know where you are.' A smell, laundered clothes straight off the washing line, a tinge of something else, cut grass. 'Wake up.' I lift my eyelids. White light pain. I squeeze them shut. 'Jesus,' I say.

'Don't be afraid. You're running out of time. Your eyes will adjust.'

Not enough time. I open my eyes again. Sting, sting, sting, blink, blink, blink, a stream of tears, stay open, stay open, blink, blink, blink, the pain eases, the room comes into a hazy view.

More blinking, more tears. I sit up and look around. All I can see is white, the walls, the ceiling, the floor, the couch I'm lying on. I'm tired. I need to sleep. I lie down again and close my eyes. The room feels warm, a safe cocoon, eiderdown duvet soft. I can feel myself floating.

'Wake up. Wake up.'

Freddie – June 1980

We were on our way to Dudley Zoo with Stuart and Louise, our first outing as a foursome. The upstairs of the bus was empty, so we piled on the back seat, me and Stuart with our feet up on the crappy brown upholstery, our backs pressed against the window, Jo-Jo and Louise in the middle, lying in-between our legs. We could see the conductor standing half-way up the stairs, watching us through the viewing mirror. A stench of cigarette smoke and dirty clothes pervaded the air like mustard gas. Stuart coughed. 'Jesus,' he said. 'It stinks back here.'

'I bet it was that four bellies bloke who got off in Bloxwich,' said Jo-Jo.

'Four bellies?' I said.

'Yeah, he barged past us. Don't tell me you didn't see him. He was as big as a tank.'

'I saw him. I've just never heard of anyone get called four bellies before.'

'She's being kind,' said Louise. 'I'd have said six.'

'Did you see the way he was walking?' said Jo-Jo. She rolled off the seat, stood up and penguin-walked half-way up the bus. Louise stood up and followed her. They turned, puffed out their cheeks and wobbled back – their bloated faces rocking under the weight of supressed laughter.

'You two are mad,' said Stuart.

'And gorgeous,' I said, pulling Jo-Jo towards me and kissing her on the lips.

Louise glared at Stuart. 'Why couldn't you say that?' she said.

'I was just about to,' he protested.

*

We took our place in the long entrance queue. I sighed. 'I can only just see the ticket office,' I said.

Jo-Jo squeezed my hand. 'Stop moaning,' she whispered. 'It'll be worth it.'

We juddered along as though we were on a faulty travellator. I could feel droplets of sweat popping on my forehead, my Adidas t-shirt was sticking to my back. A boy and a girl in front of us, both of them eating an ice-cream, started tapping each other and giggling. Their mum leaned down, took them both by the arm and said, 'If you don't behave, I'm going to feed you to the tigers.' Jo-Jo and I laughed. The children glared at us.

We reached the ticket window. 'Morning,' said the rosy-cheeked woman behind the counter. 'Lovely day, isn't it?'

'Gorgeous,' I said, handing her a ten pound note. She took the money and gave me two tickets, nodding at the two children we'd queued behind for the last twenty minutes. 'I'd get one of those ice-creams if I were you,' she said. We walked through the turnstile and waited for Stuart and Louise to pay their money.

'Shall we?' said Jo-Jo.

'What?' I said.

'Get an ice-cream. You do look hot.'

Stuart and Louise joined us. 'Where shall we go first?' said Louise.

'Freddie wants an ice-cream,' said Jo-Jo.

'Jesus,' said Stuart. 'How old are you, mate? Six.'

'It's to cool him down,' said Jo-Jo. 'Don't you want one?'

'Of course he does,' said Louise, taking Jo-Jo's arm, the pair of them walking off towards the pink and white Mr Whippy van.

*

We huddled around the site map with our 99s. I'd eaten half of my chocolate flake, pushed the rest down into the bottom of the cone and was now lightly licking my way in clockwise concentric circles around the vanilla ice-cream. 'How can you eat that so slowly?' said Jo-Jo.

'I'm making it last,' I said. 'You've just munched yours to death.'

'It's an ice-cream, Freddie. It's meant to be munched.'

I took another slow lick with the tip on my tongue, this time staring straight into Jo-Jo's eyes. 'Yummy,' I said.

She laughed.

'Shouldn't you two be getting a bed?' said Louise.

'Not when there's elephants to see,' said Jo-Jo, pointing straight in front of us.

'You didn't need to tell us,' said Stuart. 'You can smell them from here.'

Jo-Jo grabbed Louise's arm and they ran over to the elephant enclosure. Stuart and I walked over and joined them. We leaned over the three foot high wall, a two foot wide moat and twenty foot high wire net fence in front of us, and stared in silence at the two elephants and their two calves. One of the elephants reached up and pulled hay out of a basket strung high from a wooden pole. Her mouth was wide open, revealing fold after fold of fresh-pink flesh, hay being dropped in from her trunk and munched to mulch before she swallowed. The other female was standing by the man-made pool, flicking up squirts of water to clear the chalky dust from her head. The calves ambled over to join her, the baby nudging his sibling closer to the pond. 'Oh God,' said Jo-Jo. 'He's trying to push him in.'

'Here's the male,' I said.

The bull elephant charged across the dusty ground towards his herd, his gleaming tusks leading the way. He reached his family, barged straight through the middle of them, almost knocking over one of the calves, and then stood perfectly still for a few seconds, looking over at the fence. Finally, he lifted his trunk to the azure sky and trumpeted his arrival. 'Pity you can't do that,' said Jo-Jo, squeezing me around the waist.

'What makes you think I can't?' I said.

'I've not seen it so far,' she said.

'I can do that Clyde thing,' said Stuart.

We all looked at him.

'You know, the orangutan in the Clint Eastwood film.'

'You mean where he swings from the hotel bedroom light?' I said.

'That's the one,' said Stuart.

'Looks like you're in for treat,' Jo-Jo said to Louise.

'Yeah,' said Louise, looking nervously at Stuart. 'I'm glad he's warned me.'

'Shall we go and see the giraffes?' I said.

Jo-Jo and I walked off towards the giraffe house, which, according to the map, was the next stop en route and right next to Monkey World. I put my arm around Jo-Jo and squeezed her into my body. 'Your mate's a bit awkward,' she said.

I looked behind us. Stuart and Louise were following but slowly and walking apart from each other. 'I don't think they've been together that long,' I said.

'How do you know him?'

'From school. Jack knows him better than me.'

We reached the giraffes just as two of them were lolloping out into the sunshine from their covered wooden enclosure. One of the giraffes rubbed himself against the wall of the building, stretching his neck almost to the tin roof, and then started chewing on a long willowy branch that had been tied there by the keepers. The second giraffe seemed to realise he was missing out, turned around, walked back to the building and also started munching on the bark. They looked like they were kissing the wood in a slow, seductive mating ritual. Stuart and Louise joined us at the fence, but stood each side of me and Jo-Jo.

'They are ugly creatures,' said Stuart. 'It's like God had lots of bits left over and said, what do I do with these?'

'I think they're gorgeous,' said Louise.

'Me too,' said Jo-Jo. 'They're so different. That's what makes them beautiful.'

Stuart looked at me in desperation.

'I don't mind them,' I said. 'At least they've got a bit of character.'

'I need the loo,' said Louise.

'I'll come with you,' said Jo-Jo.

Stuart and I leaned on the fence and watched Jo-Jo and Louise walk away towards the toilets. 'You two okay?' I said.

'No idea. I don't seem to be able to say anything right.'

'You seemed fine earlier.'

'I know. She went all frosty after I said how I envied you being with Jo-Jo.'

I stood up and looked at him.

'I didn't mean anything by it,' he said hurriedly. 'I just meant you make a good couple, but I think she took it the wrong way.'

'A bit like most people would,' I said. 'Maybe you should apologise.'

'Yeah, sorry, mate.'

'Not to me. To Louise.'

'Maybe,' he said, looking back at the giraffes. 'Do you really like those things?'

Jo-Jo – June 1980

I pushed my strawberry lip gloss into the tight pocket of my blue denim Levi shorts and stared at myself in the mirror. We'd left

Freddie and Stuart watching the giraffes. I wondered what they were talking about. Freddie wasn't great at man-talk and I'd got the impression Stuart was a bit of a lager lout. I couldn't imagine him being Jack's friend. Perhaps I didn't know Jack well enough. The toilet flushed behind me. Louise came out of the cubicle, walked over and stood by me at the sink. She started washing her hands. I looked at her through the mirror. 'You okay?' I said.

She nodded, turned off the tap, pulled a green paper towel out of the holder, the kind that always reminded me of school, and dried her hands.

'How long have you and Stuart been going out?'

'A few weeks. How about you and Freddie?'

'It feels like forever. But we only met last November.'

'It's obvious you love each other. I don't think Stuart and I will last much longer.'

'Have you had a row? We couldn't help noticing there was an atmosphere.'

'Not really. He's just…well, compared to you two, we're not…he's not what I'm looking for.'

I waited for her to elaborate, but she scrunched up the paper towel, lobbed it into the bin and started to walk towards the door. 'We can head home if you want,' I said.

'Not before I've seen the monkeys. It'll give that prat a chance to see a real orangutan.'

I laughed. 'I think he's a bit nervous. I don't think he was serious about swinging from a light.'

'That's a pity,' she said. 'I was looking forward to that bit.'

We re-joined Freddie and Stuart just as the giraffe herd were lolloping back inside their covered enclosure. 'I think it's too hot for them,' said Freddie.

'Shall we head to the monkey house?' I said.

'Good idea,' said Stuart. 'They're my favourites.'

Louise and I looked at each other and burst out laughing.

'What?' said Stuart. 'They are.'

'Come on, mate,' said Freddie, putting his hand on Stuart's back. 'I think it's a private joke.'

*

The queue to get inside the monkey house ran along the wire net fence, which meant we could pass the time by watching the tribe of six chimpanzees lying moribund on the grass in the mid-day sun. One of them, it looked like the alpha male, was flat on his back, slightly apart from the rest of the group, arm over his eyes, one leg raised and the other crossed over it. We could hear him snoring and breaking wind. 'Looks like he's sleeping off last night's beer,' said Stuart.

'Typical man,' said Louise. 'One sniff of the barman's apron, a bit of sun and he's good for nothing.'

'Could be worse,' I said. 'You could be lying next to him.'

The queue edged forward, the pong of ammonia raising up in notches of pungency as we moved closer to the door. Two of the chimpanzees lifted their heads at exactly the same time, threw their arms around each other, cuddled and stroked each other's faces. One of the other chimps sat up, edged over to the cuddling pair and flopped on her back in submissive pose with her legs up and wide open.

'Okay,' said Freddie, a toothy grin spread across his face. 'It feels like we should stop watching now.'

The queue moved forward just as the cuddling two were separating and eagerly moving towards the legs up monkey. I looked at Freddie. 'There are children watching,' I whispered. 'Some of them are taking pictures.'

'They probably think it's a game,' he said. 'Which it is, sort of.'

I turned around to look at Stuart and Louise. Stuart was rubbernecking to see the monkeys, the movement of the queue having stolen his vantage point. Louise was staring at me, her cheeks flushed. 'He, is so embarrassing,' she said.

'What?' said Stuart, turning back towards us. 'You've got to admit it's funny. You can't take your eyes off them. Dirty buggers.'

Louise slapped him on the arm and laughed. 'You needn't get any ideas,' she said.

*

As we walked into the monkey house, I grabbed Freddie's arm and pulled him back towards me. He gave me a quizzical look and I nodded at the young couple in front of us who were posing against the viewing glass, arms wrapped around each other, for their picture to be taken by an older man who was wearing a tweed Grandad cap. 'You nearly walked across their shot,' I said.

'Sorry,' said Freddie, putting up his hand to the couple. 'She's always telling me off for that.'

'Not that he takes a blind bit of notice,' I said.

'Jesus,' said Stuart, walking up behind us. 'It stinks of piss in here.'

'What did you expect?' said Louise.

'Yeah,' said Freddie. 'They don't exactly have en-suite.'

'Mind you,' I said. 'That's a bit out of order.'

All of their eyes followed my gaze towards the ceiling of the first enclosure where a red-haired orangutan was hanging upside down from a tyre and urinating a golden shower onto the concrete floor below. The urine splashed and pooled, narrowly missing a troop of gambolling and grooming chimpanzees.

'It's never ending,' said Louise.

'How great would that be?' said Stuart. 'Just pissing on everyone from the roof.'

'I'm not sure that bus conductor would be impressed,' said Freddie. 'He wasn't happy with us putting our feet on the seats.'

The shower stopped and the orangutan let out a scream. He turned the right way up, grabbed one of the ropes hanging next to the tyre and swung across to the other side of the roof, where he perched on one of the many branches fixed by the keepers to the walls of the enclosure. He reached over his shoulder with his lanky arm and scratched his back.

'He looks pleased with himself,' said Freddie.

'Yeah,' I said. 'He's not hung around the scene of the crime for long though.'

'You should never shit on your own doorstep,' said Stuart.

'It all looks really sad,' said Louise. 'Concrete floors and nailed on branches. Where's nature in all of that?'

'They look happy enough,' said Stuart.

'They've not got much choice,' said Freddie.

'Come on,' I said. 'Let's see what's next door.'

Freddie, Stuart and I walked forward, but Louise didn't move. She was still staring into the enclosure. I looked at Stuart. He turned back to Louise and put his arm through hers. 'He's fine,' he said, nodding at the grinning ape.

'There's a donation box at the entrance,' she said. 'It might help.'

'Okay,' he said, smiling. 'We'll sort it on the way out.' He put his arm around her and they joined Freddie and me at the next enclosure.

'Macaque monkeys,' said Freddie, reading from the wooden plaque screwed to the wall. 'I can't see them,' he said, peering through the glass.

'Me neither,' I said. 'How come there are so many bushes and plants in here and next door was like a cell?'

'I guess it's because these are a bit timid and like to hide,' said Freddie. 'Whereas your man next door doesn't care who sees him.'

'There they are,' said Louise, pointing to the top of the enclosure.

I looked up. There were two black monkeys cuddled together high in the branches, their wide, dewy eyes staring straight back at us. 'Oh God,' I said. 'They look terrified.' One of the monkeys shifted position slightly, pulling apart from the other, and there, suckling a nipple on the second monkey's chest, his eyes closed to the world, was an infant. The first monkey seemed to realise his mistake and moved back into his original position, cuddling the second one close, hiding the baby from view once more.

'That is so sweet,' said Louise.

'Yes it is,' said Stuart. 'They're almost human.'

Jo-Jo – June 1989

We were in the Saleem Bagh curry house in Cannock. I ordered a vegetable bhuna, Stuart had the beef madras and Louise had the tandoori mix with lamb, chicken and seekh kebabs. 'It's a pity Jason couldn't make it,' said Louise, tearing off a piece of her garlic naan bread.

'Not unusual though,' said Stuart. 'We've only met the bloke once and that was accidental when we were out shopping. I don't think he likes us.'

'It's not you,' I said. 'He's shy. He doesn't mean anything by it. Anyway, someone's got to look after Amy.'

'Yeah,' said Louise. 'Not everyone's as full of themselves as you.'

'It's only a curry,' said Stuart, wiping his forehead and blowing his nose on the white cloth napkin.

'How come I always finish up apologising for you?' said Louise.

'How old's that sprog of yours?' said Stuart, totally ignoring the question.

'Five,' I said. 'They grow up so fast don't they?'

Louise glanced nervously at Stuart.

'You're not, are you?' I said.

'Yep,' said Stuart, squeezing Louise's hand. 'It finally happened.'

I stood up and hugged them both. 'Oh God,' I said. 'I'm so pleased for you. I know how much you've wanted this.'

'We're not there yet,' said Stuart. 'We've got to wrap her in cotton wool until Superman arrives.'

'Her?' said Louise. 'Who's her? The cat's mother.'

'You. I mean you. You know what I mean.'

'And what's with the Superman. I'm having a Superwoman.' I laughed.

'What?' said Louise.

'You two,' I said. 'You bickered like that the first time I met you.'

'At the zoo,' said Stuart. 'You were with Freddie. Do you ever hear from him now?'

'Do you?' I said. 'He was your mate.'

He shook his head. 'I saw Jack a few years ago.'

'You know,' said Louise. 'I'd have put my house on you and Freddie making it. We were gobsmacked when you split up.'

'Me too,' I said. 'These things happen I suppose.'

'His loss,' said Stuart, mopping up the madras sauce with his chapatti.

'Yes,' I said. 'His loss. I'll tell you one thing, I wouldn't have bet a dog kennel on you two making it through the trip to the zoo, let alone beyond.'

'Me neither,' said Louise, glaring at Stuart. 'Do you have to eat like that?'

'Like what?' he said.

'Slapping your chops. No-one wants to see inside your mouth.'

Freddie – August 2015

I'm clutching a bottle of Jack Daniels in my left hand, the steps of the ladder are blurring in and out of view, tears stream down my face, my nose is bunged with snot, my head feels as though it's cracked across the scalp. I flick on the light switch, dump the uncapped whisky bottle on the boards and haul myself inside the loft, spittle dripping from my mouth. I look around at my setup. A cottage oak dining chair, Edwardian antique, really uncomfortable to sit on, a polyester rope hanging down next to it, already secured to the beam. I take a last swig of whisky, climb onto the chair and place the noose around my neck. I hesitate and draw my hand across my face to wipe away the sweat and sobs. I pull the knot tight and start to shuffle on the chair, one rock left, one rock right, backwards, forwards. I can feel the chair going from under me…

Springsteen's harmonica.

For a moment I stayed in the dream – the whisky, the noose, the rocking chair. I could feel my heartbeat in my ears. I opened my eyes, reached over, turned off the alarm and lay back with my hands behind my head and stared at the artex ceiling. 'Jesus,' I said. Tai, my little black cat, who was lying at the end of the bed, lifted her head and blinked at me. 'I've got no choice,' I said to her. 'You'll be okay with Jack.' I turned out of bed, surprised at how calm I felt, and walked out of the bedroom, across the landing to the shower.

Half an hour later, I was sitting at my kitchen table, a cold mug of coffee pushed to one side, four boxes of the ten milligram Propranolol in front of me, a glass of water already poured. I'd popped sixteen of the round purple tablets from the two strips in the first box. I picked up my phone. I realised I should call Jack, say goodbye properly, but I didn't know how to start the conversation. I put the phone down and reached for the tablets.

*

'Freddie. Freddie.'

Jack's voice. He was shaking me. I wanted to wake up, but my eyelids wouldn't lift.

'Freddie. Freddie.'

His shaking was getting harder. 'Wake up. For God's sake. How many of these have you taken?'

I opened my eyes. It felt like I was looking through slits. He was leaning over me. I raised my head, which felt too big for my shoulders, and wiped the saliva from the corner of my mouth. I felt drunk, but it was the haze from the beta-blockers. 'I'm not sure,' I mumbled, staring through fog at the tablets. 'A box,' I think.

'Jesus,' he said.

I dropped my head back on the table and closed my eyes again. Seconds later I heard him say, 'An ambulance, please. I think my friend's taken an overdose.'

'I want to die, Jack,' I said.

Freddie – June 1970 – Cowboy Dreams

We were lying on the grass in King George's – John Wayne and Audie Murphy. I spat once, pushed my black Stetson back on my head and squinted into the distance. I mimicked a gun shot, threw a puff-ball of dust behind us and pushed him to the ground. 'I thought you said they were miles away,' I said.

'We're too open here,' he said.

'Over there,' I said. 'That cabin.'

'It's too far. I'm not moving.'

I rolled to his side. 'We owe it the others, partner. Where's your loyalty?'

'I don't want to die.'

'You think they did. Staying here we die.'

I whistled another bullet and pushed him down again. 'They've found their range. We need to go now.'

'Okay. I'll follow you.'

'That clump of conifers, first base.'

I bounced to my feet and started running, head down, weaving left, right, left, my toy Colt 45 still in my holster. I stumbled, went onto my knees, got back up and danced a cowboy hop across the grass, sounding death warrant bullets, pretending they were pinging at my shiny plastic cowboy boots. I skidded a dust slide into the trees, panting, my heart banging out of my chest. 'Come on,' I shouted. 'Get out of there.'

He appeared, the brim of his hat pulled low, his gun drawn, firing bullets out of his Colt like a demented wasp.

'For God's sake, run. What the hell are you shooting at?'

He fell.

'No,' I screamed, getting onto my knees.

'I'm okay,' he said, getting back on his feet, his gun lost, sprinting, weaving like a gazelle outthinking a lion. He was nearly there. Another ping, another, another. He skidded beside me. A Cheshire-wide grin. 'God, that felt good,' he yelled to the sky.

'What were you shooting at?' I said.

'Anything. Didn't feel right just running.'

'But they're too far away.'

'They're shooting at us.'

'With rifles. It's different.' I looked at the horizon, mimicked a hail of bullets and pushed him to the ground. 'I think we might have wound them up a bit, but we're nearly at the cabin. We can re-group there.'

'That might be pushing our luck.'

'We have no choice, brother.'

'It's all right for you,' he said, patting his stomach. 'I'm not exactly built for speed.'

'You'll be fine.'

'Famous last words. It's always the chubby guy who gets it.' He rolled onto his back and puffed out his cheeks. 'I've done my bit. I need a horse.'

'Do you see any horses?'

'Yeah, well –'

'– Hang on a minute. Why have they stopped shooting?'

We made another scan of the horizon.

'You see it?' I said, the sun stinging my eyes.

'I see it.'

'How many?'

'Six or seven. Riding hard.'

'This is our chance.'

'They'll have left a gun on us.'

We looked at the sanctuary of the bandstand, five hundred yards of open ground away. I whistled the sound of a bullet zinging into the bushes and we hit dirt again. 'They can't have left more than one, two at the most.'

'I've already told you, I don't want to die.'

'We'll run together. They're getting closer by the second. There's rifles in the cabin.'

'I've got a wife and kids.'

I patted him on the back. 'And you'll see them again, my friend, if we keep our nerve.'

'You'll stay with me?'

'Every step.'

He looked up at the cloudless sky, crossed himself and squeezed my arm. 'Let's do it.'

'After three…'

'Run. For god's sake, run.'

A ping off a rock, another off a fallen branch, another…

He crumpled. 'I'm hit.'

I skidded to a halt, turned back. 'I'm coming, buddy. Hold on.' I reached him 'You okay?'

'My arm.'

Two more shots. He grabbed his thigh, screamed, and looked at me. 'I'm bleeding bad,' he said. 'Leave me. Save yourself.'

I dragged him to his feet. 'Come on. We're nearly there.'

Ping, ping, ping…

We put our arms around each other, limping and weaving. 'Come on, man. We can do this.'

Ping, ping, ping…

He fell, pushed me forwards. 'Go on. Leave me.'

'No chance.'

I dragged him up again, more limping, more weaving, nearly there, nearly there. We jumped onto the bandstand, dropped to the floor and laughed. 'That was brilliant,' I screamed.

'Best yet.'

'What was all that about your wife and kids?'

Jack lifted his hat and wiped his brow. 'It's what cowboys say, partner.'

Freddie – August 2015

'So, he's going to be okay.'

'He's going to be fine. Just sleepy for the next twenty-four hours. He's only taken about eighty milligrams. Some people take that every day.'

I could hear the conversation, machines were beeping. I could smell antiseptic. Someone was holding my hand. 'Jack,' I said, opening my eyes. He let go of my hand.

'I'll leave you to it,' said the nurse. She turned to me. 'I'll come back and check you later.'

'Thank you,' said Jack.

'She seems nice,' I said, stretching my legs down the bed, crunching over the nylon sheets.

'She's pissed with you. They've got enough to do with people who are ill. What were you thinking of?'

'I wasn't.'

'It's becoming a habit, Freddie. First the train, now this…'

I started crying. 'It's all right for you, Jack. With your perfect life.'

He held my hand again. 'It's okay,' he said. 'We'll talk later.'

Let's get you out of here and back to mine. At least if we're under the same roof I can keep an eye on you and not feel the need to pop round every five minutes to check you're still breathing.'

I closed my eyes again.

*

I was lying in a single bed in Jack's spare room, snuggled under a white Jeff Banks duvet – the cat's room he called it. On the walls were the framed pictures that Jack had said he couldn't hang anywhere else in the house – a framed copy of John Lennon's *Shaved Fish* album, 'Woman is the Nigger of the World' jumping out of the track list. Even in the early seventies, Lennon was pilloried for using the N word, but he brushed it off, saying only the white 'right on' people were getting offended. Next to that hung an original framed *Pulp Fiction* film poster that Jack had tracked down on e-bay and bought from a cinema in Copenhagen. The headline said, '*simpelthen et mestervaerk*' (simply a masterpiece); the picture was Uma Thurman drawing on a cigarette and holding a smoking gun.

The bedroom door opened. 'Oh good,' said Jack. 'You're awake. I've brought you a cup of tea.'

I sat up and rested the back of my head against the headboard.

He put the tea on the bedside cabinet and sat down on the edge of the bed. 'How are you feeling?' he said.

'Knackered.'

'I'm not surprised. You slept okay though?'

'Yeah. This bed's really comfortable. No wonder the cats like it.'

'Do you feel up to talking?'

I knew it was coming. I was surprised he'd held it inside for twenty-four hours. Neither of us had said a word on the way back from the hospital, but you could feel the tension of the unanswered questions simmering away inside the Mini. 'I don't know what to say to you, Jack.'

'You could start by telling me why. I thought you were okay after we'd talked at the boat yard.'

'So did I, but I couldn't see any other way.'

'Killing yourself isn't the answer. I thought we were friends.'

'We are, best friends, but you've got Bob and, well, I just keep fucking everything up.'

'What am I going to do with you?'

'Give me a best friend hug.'

'I ought to punch you.'

'I'd prefer the hug, and you are a Social Worker.'

'Okay,' he said, smiling. 'But this doesn't mean I fancy you.'

'You've already told me that.'

He gave me a puzzled look.

'When I asked you to kiss me in Sitges.'

'Jesus, Freddie. That was years ago. And you were drunk.'

'You turned me down.'

'Well, I've always had my standards,' he said, pulling me towards him and hugging me close. 'Call me next time. I don't want to lose you.'

Something splattered against the bedroom window. Jack let go of me, stood up and walked over to look down into the back garden. 'A crow,' he said. 'Damn thing's landed on the patio. I'll have to get it up before Boris skins it and leaves it on the lounge carpet.' He looked back at me. 'What do you want to do about Jo-Jo?'

'I can't imagine she'll want to see me now.'

'Do you want to see her? After what she told you.'

'I keep telling you, Jack. It's not her fault. It's mine.'

'It's just life, Freddie. Do you want to see her?'

'I can't call her.'

'You don't have to,' he said. 'She called you. She's coming round tomorrow.'

'You've spoken to her.'

'I went to see her this morning. Her and Amy.'

'You've told her what happened.'

'She has a right to know, Freddie. You just left her. She was worried about you.'

'I don't know if I can speak to her.'

'No choice, mate. Listen, I'm going to sort that bird.'

'I am sorry, Jack. You must think I'm a right pain in the arse.'

'Same as it ever was,' he said, walking out of the bedroom.

Jo-Jo – August 2015

A memory – I'm ten, it's mid-November and I'm lying in bed listening to Mum and Dad talking in low pitched voices on the stairs. 'Come back to bed, love. It's two o'clock in the morning.'

'But he's out there, Joseph. I can hear him. He needs me.' I creep out onto the landing and sit on the top step, my back against the wall. I can see Dad's pyjama covered back and feel the cold draft blowing into the house through the open front door.

'There's no-one there, love,' pleads Dad. 'Come inside. You'll catch your death.'

'No,' screams Mum. 'He's here on the front lawn. He's lost his mummy. Don't you care? What's wrong with you?'

Another evening, around the same time, Mum gathers us around the kitchen table and tells us about a man, dressed in a suit and tie, who had visited her in the middle of the night, sat at the end of her bed and told her fairy stories about children being cut in half by slathering ogres and flee-ridden witches. Josh is seven. Dad stands up half-way through the story. 'Come on,' he says to me and Josh.

'No, Joseph,' says Mum. 'They need to hear this. He's coming back.'

'No they don't,' says Dad, pushing us out of the kitchen.

Mum's uninvited schizophrenia lodger shared our house all the way through my childhood, her delusions making us tip-toe around in her fantasy world. She was convinced she looked after the house and all of us single-handedly – 'It wouldn't hurt one of you to have a go.' 'No-one ever thanks me.' 'Can someone make me a cup of tea for a change?' In reality, Dad cooked it, Dad cleaned it, and we all colluded with Mum's addled perception – all of us walking in ill-fitting shoes in case we upset her. It was easier than drowning in the blue whale weight of her depressive mood. She'd take to her bed for weeks on end, smothered under her duvet, locked away with her voices, no-one able to reach her. She must have been in pain. She must have been tormented. I should have tried harder to understand.

*

'Your destination is on the right,' said the Mazda's sat nav.

'It means left,' said Amy, pointing at Jack's Mini. 'There's number twenty-two. You'll have to park over the road.'

I pulled into the only space, turned off the engine and looked at the house with its lush, perfectly mown front lawn, red-rose-bed-borders, all in perfect bloom, not a hint of greenfly in sight, all edged to slide rule standard. I smiled. Jack's OCD was still alive and kicking.

'You ready?' said Amy.

'I just hope he's ready for us.'

'Jack said he wanted to see you.'

'I'm not sure he'll want the audience though.'

'You think I should wait in the car.'

'No. I want you with me. At least to start with. Let's see what Jack does.'

She hugged me. 'It'll be fine,' she said.

We unfastened our seatbelts, got out of the car and walked across the road hand in hand. As we reached the pavement, the front door opened. Jack smiled at us from the step. 'You found it okay then,' he said.

'The joy of sat nav,' I said.

'Freddie's in the lounge. I've bunked him up in the spare room for a few days.'

'Mum was wondering if we ought to leave them to it,' said Amy. 'Perhaps you and I should go out.'

'We don't want to throw you out of your own house,' I said. Jack laughed. 'Happy to go for a coffee, Amy. If you fancy it.'

'Will you be okay, Mum?'

'Of course,' I said. 'Me and Freddie need to talk.'

Jack grabbed a denim coat off one of the coat hooks in the hallway and offered Amy his arm. 'There's a good place not far away,' he said. 'We can walk there.'

Amy hugged me again. 'I'll be back in an hour,' she said.

'The lounge is on the left,' said Jack as they walked down the path. 'I've made the coffee. Freddie knows where everything else is.'

I closed the door behind me, took a deep breath and walked down the hallway.

Freddie – August 2015

A memory – the unshaven doctor, eyes weighed down with puffy bags, gives us Mum's death sentence. I leave her bedside at the Manor Hospital in Walsall, walk out to the waiting area, get a plastic cup of machine coffee and load it with sugar to kill the taste. Terry Wogan's radio show is being broadcast through a set of Toshiba speakers someone has set up over the entrance door. I stare out at the hospital car park, all of the cars are covered in a smattering of snow. 'It's too cold to snow,' I hear one of the nurses say. 'Tell that to the Arctic,' says her mate, 'They've got bucket loads of the stuff.' There's a Christmas tree in the far corner of the waiting area, which has been decorated in white candle lights and red baubles. A peg fairy has been plonked on the tree's summit. She's too heavy for the branch, making it lean over, dragging the fairy off-centre, making her look like she has already started on the Christmas sherry. I sit down on one of the hard plastic chairs. Cancer. A taboo word in our family, talked about in hushed tones, dropped voices, none of us wanting to run the risk of saying the word too loud. Even thinking about it is dangerous. A memory: I'm ten, a kid in our street, Nicky Farmer, dies. 'Banged himself on a wall,' says Mum. 'Bruise didn't come out. Gave him cancer. You be careful.' A memory: spending the rest of my life worrying over every knock, every no-show bruise. Asbestosis. A variant on a theme. Another banned word. One contracting job painting the inside of a cooling tower lined with blue asbestos and Dad is dead at forty-five. A memory: fully expecting to die at forty-five, the shock, surprise, the *what do I do now* feeling when I reach forty-six. A memory: holding my breath when I enter a building that I've been told is lined with asbestos cladding. All of it is Dad's legacy. I stop myself from thinking about him. This is Mum's diagnosis, Mum's death. He isn't going to take over. I ask the doctor if Mum is in pain. He says no. I don't believe him. All I want to do is get her home. It will all be okay at home. Wogan introduces what he says is one of his favourite songs, 'Me and the Elephant' by Gene Cotton. It reminds me of Jo-Jo and our trip to the zoo.

Freddie – July 1997

Hotel Romantico, Sitges – I was lying on a sun lounger at the side of the pool, pretending to read J.K. Rowling's *Harry Potter and the Philosopher's Stone*. Jack had gone off on the train to Barcelona, saying he was fed up of me moaning about the hotel owner, a Super Mario lookalike, real name Dimitri. Mario's wife, who behaved like a Latin Cybil Fawlty, used to elongate her husband's name when she called him, de-MEE-tree, de-MEE-tree, repeating it over and over. Eventually, he'd charge off from behind the reception desk, sometimes mid-conversation, find his wife wherever she was resting, usually in the gardens, and they'd have an excitable exchange between them in Spanish. Minutes later, he'd reappear, irritable and growling at the guests. On our second day, I'd asked if I could change my room. 'You don't like my rooms?' he snapped.

'Yes,' I said. 'I just wondered if there was a chance of a room nearer to the pool.'

'Fine,' he said, waving a dismissive hand. 'I find you a new room. Be so close to pool, jump in pool off balcony.' He fell out with me and Jack because we didn't eat in his restaurant or stay in the bar for his evening entertainment. 'I do this for you, not for me. For you to enjoy.' Feeling guilty, we went to the bar the following evening and watched a Roy Chubby Brown impersonator slaughter Smokie's 'Living Next Door to Alice.' Later that evening, we walked up to the reception desk to collect our room keys. 'You had good evening?' said Mario.

'It was very good,' said Jack.

'Bravo, bravo, bravo,' said Mario, doing a little jig at the back of his counter. '

All right, mate' I said. 'There's no need to take the piss.'

'That's your fault,' said Jack as we walked towards the lift.

We'd stopped going to the beach because of the nudist couple Jack had nicknamed Bertha and Buddha. He'd start to get prickly as soon as they walked past us, Bertha wrapped in a full length sarong and wearing a wide-brimmed blue straw hat; Buddha in his fluorescent yellow Nike beach shorts, their thighs slapping together as they headed for the partial seclusion of the rocks. 'Here's the roly-polies,' Jack would whisper to me from behind his Clive Barker novel. What really annoyed him was the way Bertha greeted him with a cheery good morning. 'No shame,' he'd say after he'd said good morning back. Buddha had an all over shiny conker tan, moobs the size of footballs and a completely bald head that looked too small for his hairless body. Jack would sit up on his beach towel, resting on his elbows, and watch them settle in their chosen spot, Bertha opening up her sarong, walking to the water's edge and bending over to dip her hand to check the temperature, revealing her cellulite buttocks to the world – 'walnut butt' Jack called it. It all became too much when a short-less Buddha rolled over on his towel and Jack said he saw the great man's flaccid penis flop to a new side. 'No-one wants to see that,' he said, picking up his towel. 'Come on. We'll get a sun lounger by the pool.' '

Stop looking,' I said. 'They're doing no harm.'

'You can't miss them, Freddie. They're putting me off my lunch.'

Being away from the beach meant people watching at the hotel. On one of the sun loungers was the man Jack and I had nicknamed the Major. He had a white handlebar moustache and used to stand with his hands behind his back, holding a G&T, surveying the guests like a military commander observing his troops at the end of a day's battle. His wife would tell him off if he hadn't put on the right swimming trunks, the ones to match her outfit, and send him back to their room to change. She'd roll her eyes at us. 'Men,' she'd say. 'I don't how you manage to get up in a morning.' Next to them was the couple from Bradford who had a fluorescent pink duck inflatable that nearly filled the pool. They came on a hotel unknown, cheap deal and complained to the rep as soon as they arrived – 'You've got to move us from these old fogeys,' she said, pointing around the sun loungers before quickly adding, 'No offence, everyone.' And then there was the Italian couple. Him, an Adonis; her, Helen of Troy. They would lie face to face looking into each other's eyes, him, stroking her arm, applying regular top-ups of sunblock to her back; her, forever straightening his jet black hair and resting her hand on his bare thigh. Every so often, they'd disappear to their room for half-an-hour. Jack would nudge me when this happened. 'They've gone to release the pressure,' he'd say. One day, Helen was sitting on the pool steps reading her book when the gate to the annexe hotel opened and a new family, Dad, Mum and two children, a boy and a girl, walked into the pool area clutching their towels. The girl, who was about eleven, saw the pool and screamed in a black country accent, 'Oh my God.' She dropped her towel, ran towards the water and jumped in the deep end with a cry of, 'Jeronimo', sending up a tidal wave and drenching Helen, turning her book into a sodden pulp. Jeronimo came to the surface, wiped her face and shouted towards her mum and dad, 'That was great. I'm gonna do it again.' Everyone looked at each other, stood up and pulled their sun lounger a bit further away from the pool's edge.

Jo-Jo – February 1990

I was in a wine bar on a rare night out with Karen. She was slow dancing with a bushy-bearded Australian waiter who had been chatting to her between orders all evening. He'd finished his shift an hour ago and in that time they'd consumed most of the bottle of Merlot he'd brought with him when he'd perched on the stool next to her. Jenifer Rush's 'Power of Love' had started up, which prompted Karen to scream, 'Oh, I love this song,' and drag him onto the dance floor. I was watching them dance, their legs interlocked, slow rhythmic swaying from the hips. They were standing up, with their clothes on, but definitely making love. The couples around them were giving out nervous sideways glances. Some stopped dancing and went back to their tables. 'Your friend looks like she's enjoying herself,' said a voice beside me. I turned around.

'Scott,' said the man sitting on the bar stool next to me. 'Can I get you a drink?'

I pointed at my wine glass, which was over half full. 'I'm good, thanks,' I said.

He nodded at the dance floor. 'How about a dance?'

'I'm married,' I said, holding up the third finger on my left hand to show him the eighteen karat gold band.

'Does that stop you dancing?' he said, holding out his hand.

That's when I should have made my excuses, but I hadn't been out in months. I looked at him, Scott, my new bar companion. He was clean shaven, which bucked the trend of the designer stubble doing the rounds, had blond shoulder length hair, blue eyes, and was dressed in what looked like a very expensive navy blue suit, probably designer, with a white shirt. He reminded me of Joey out of the sitcom *Bread*. 'Just one dance,' I said, taking his hand.

We walked onto the dance floor as Jenifer was fading out and Rod Stewart's 'First Cut is the Deepest' started up. We started swaying to the music, his hands resting gently on the bottom of my back. I could smell his Kouros aftershave. 'I know it's only one dance,' he said, 'but do I get to know your name?'

Jo-Jo – March 1990

It was eleven o'clock in the morning and we were lying in bed, our third time at the same hotel, staying in what Scott called a dayroom. 'Hotels let you do that?' I said when he suggested it.

'Of course. Wedding parties do it all the time.'

'But we're not a wedding party. Have you done this sort of thing before?'

'No. But I've got friends who have.' We used to meet in the car park at eight forty-five exactly, ready to occupy our nine to five room, the hotel staff smiling at each other knowingly as we booked in, taking full-payment on arrival. Scott used to come prepared with what he called his 'Scooby snacks' – first time, ham and tomato sandwiches until he found out I was vegetarian and then he brought tuna to go with the plain crisps, tomato juice and a flask of coffee.

'I don't get why you can't leave him,' said Scott.

'I can't just walk out. What about Amy?'

He was looking up at the ceiling, his one hand behind his head. I was lying on his hairless chest. I didn't know men could have bald chests. I assumed it was something to do with him being blond.

'You could take her with you.'

'He'd never let that happen. Anyway, I couldn't break up her family.'

He sighed, rolled from underneath me and got out of bed.

'You okay?' I said.

'I need the loo,' he said, walking off towards the bathroom.

I wondered, not for the first time, what I was doing, risking everything for a dayroom liaison and now he was talking about going away for a weekend to Oxford. I'd get caught. People who have affairs always get caught. I heard the toilet flush and he walked out of the bathroom and climbed back into bed. He squeezed me close. I felt a tingle of electric charge shoot through my body. His touch, being held by him, it was something I hadn't felt since…

'You know,' he said. 'We could make this work.'

'What do you mean?'

'Take it to the next level, turn us into a proper couple.'

'We're okay, aren't we, as we are?'

'I'm just saying if you ever wanted to.'

I lifted my head, pulled myself up his body and kissed him on the lips. 'Let's just have some fun for a while, see what happens.'

He returned my kiss. 'Talking of fun,' he said.

*

'Dear Jo-Jo,
I'm missing you and you've only been away half an hour. I wish I could wash away our pasts and it

34

just be me and you. Each day I'm with you, I can see it drawing you back. I know that very soon you will be gone, your guilt and love for Amy stopping you living your own life. I don't blame you. It's a part of you that makes you a very special person. I know you don't want to hurt anyone, but that's not real life. Someone always gets hurt. If you're still seeing me for that reason, please don't. I'll survive. I love you very much, but it has to be returned for the right reasons. I don't want us to end up hating each other. I never want that to happen. I don't think we can ever be a normal couple, shopping, cooking, planning a holiday. I think for you that's a commitment you've already made and it's painful, for your daughter's sake, to even think about doing those things with me. How you'll ever have any sort of life with anyone else, to be honest, I don't think you will, and I think it will have to be a very special person to accept what you're offering. I'll always remember us, the excitement, the secrecy, the snatched moments, the long phone conversations and, yes, the empty feeling in the pit of my stomach every time you return to your marriage.

I feel so alone and scared sometimes. I don't want to be a bit on the side, your knock off. I could give you so much love, if you'd let me. I do try to be what you want me to be, but it's hard for me not to show what I feel. I need to stop thinking about you so much.

See you next week.
All my love
Your crazy man Xxx x'

*

We were sitting on a public bench opposite the entrance to Magdalene College in Oxford, eating cheese and pickle sandwiches, drinking tomato juice, watching the cyclists and walkers, who we assumed were students, as they rushed past us and into the college, most of them travelling in pairs. 'First thing you do, I guess,' said Scott.

'What?' I said.

'Find yourself a lover when you get to university. Makes the time go quicker.'

'Is that what you did?'

'I didn't go. Not something you did where I come from.'

'I went and it wasn't the first thing I did.'

'You went to Uni?'

'You don't have to sound so surprised.'

'Sorry, it's just, well, like I said, not many people from my background do. What did you study?'

'English Lit. I went to Lincoln. That's where I met Jason.'

'Proves my point.'

'He wasn't a student. He was one of the lecturers.'

'You had an affair with your teacher?'

I could feel a growl of irritation starting in my stomach. Sometimes, outside of the hotel bedroom, being with him felt like I was out with a child. We were the same biological age, but there was an aeon of maturity gap. I looked at him, his face smeared in a smutty grin. I imagined a Sid James laugh reverberating around his head. I was starting to feel like his mum, which, given what we'd been doing an hour ago, felt wrong. He saw the expression on my face and stopped smiling. 'I met him at a party,' I said. 'He didn't teach on my course and neither of us were in a relationship. His wife had died years earlier. He was kind at a time when I needed someone to be kind.' I could hear the tone of my voice, clipped, like Miss Moir, my senior school deputy headmistress.

'Sorry,' he said. 'I didn't mean to annoy you.'

'You haven't,' I said, squeezing his hand. 'It's just, it was a bad time in my life. I don't how we got onto the subject.'

'Lovers at university. I didn't know you'd met Jason there. He must be a lot older than you if he was a lecturer. That explains a lot.'

'It doesn't explain anything. The age difference isn't what's wrong with our marriage.'

*

I parked up in a lay-by, just along the lane from the church in Buildwas. He pulled his car behind my Nissan Sunny and flashed his lights to announce his arrival. I watched him through the door mirror. He got out of his car, locked it and walked up to my car. I wound down my window. 'Your car or mine,' he said.

'My car or yours for what?'

'You know. To get comfy. We could use the Cortina. The seats go right back.'

'Sounds like you're an expert.'

'No, it's just…'

'There's no way I'm having cramped sex in a car, Scott.'

'That's not what I suggested.'

'It's what you meant though.'

I wound up the window, got out of the car, locked it and walked off across the lane. 'Let's go for a walk.'

'A walk?'

I turned around and held out my hand. 'Yes, a walk.'

'Oh, I get you. A walk.'

We climbed over the three bar, ranch style fence and walked through the trees, emerging into a farmer's field. We stood and stared at the openness, which stretched out and out and out to the horizon. 'Imagine owning all of this,' said Scott.

'It's beautiful,' I said. 'Uncluttered. Helps you clear your head. Come on. Let's lie down over there. I want to look at the clouds.'

'Course you do,' he said.

I lay on the grass. Scott knelt beside me. I put my hand behind my head and looked up at the sky. He leaned down and went to kiss me. I put my finger on his lips. 'I really do want to look at the clouds.'

He sighed and lay down.

'Now,' I said. 'You need to look for a cloud that looks like a face and say which celebrity it reminds you of.'

'Do we have to do this, Jo-Jo?'

'Yes, it's fun. Look. That one there. It looks like Freddie Mercury. Don't you think?'

'No, it looks like all of the other clouds.' He sat up again. 'I'd really like to kiss you,' he said.

'Okay,' I said. 'If you're not going to play my cloud game, you can kiss me.'

*

'Dear Jo-Jo,

If you're reading this, it means I've been strong enough to see through the hardest thing I've ever done. If you only knew the times in the past few days I've wavered, thinking what the hell, then I've thought about it and know it's the right way. But God, it hurts. I can't bear to see your face when you speak of Amy, the raw pain brought on by guilt. I can't compete with that. All I can give you is my love, and that's not enough. Don't be sorry, I wouldn't have missed loving you for anything. You have given me something no-one can take away. The experiences we've shared, the fun we've had. I wouldn't change a minute. If only we'd met at another time, perhaps we might have had a chance.

Be strong, sort yourself out, and if, by a slim chance, you find it's not what you want, that you can't slot back to the way it should be, I'll be here. All you need is to be certain, and do it for the right reasons. I couldn't go through this pain again. I will be okay. I need to sort myself out, find out what I really want.

Well, I'm rambling on again as usual and probably not saying the right things, but you know me with words. All I know is it's going to be hard not having you around.

Perhaps one day I'll take a walk down to our field in Buildwas, where I think for me I fell in love with you first. Anyway, I think what I'm really trying to say is, you might not be here but you'll always be in my heart. I'll always love you.

Your crazy man Xxx x'

Jo-Jo – July 1990

Me and Scott were walking on the beach in Cleethorpes, past the boating lake, the Humberston Fitties, the air filled with screeching gullies looking for chips along the prom, side-stepping mounds of sand put there by lugworms. Scott squeezed my hand and nodded towards the horizon. 'That beach goes on forever. Do you think the sea's still there?'

Two women walked past us, heading in the opposite direction, roll upon roll of fat squeezed up, out and over their boob tubes and tight fitting beach shorts. They smiled at Scott over their 99 ice-creams and then giggled to each other as they passed us. 'Looks like you've pulled,' I said.

'Did you see the state?' he said.

'Fat lasses,' I said. 'They need the layers. It gets cold up here in the winter.'

We carried on walking. A blonde haired girl, aged about seven, in a bright pink swimming costume, and a man in swim shorts covered in penguin motifs came towards us, the man, in front, the little girl, stepping out behind. 'What are you doing, Chloe?' said the man, turning his head.

'I'm walking in your footsteps, Dad,' she said. 'But your strides are so big.' It resurfaced my memories of Dad, his bear hugs, his sixth sense that always told him where I was, how I was feeling, but that had all changed with his tart. I focussed on the horizon, trying to push everything else out of my head.

'Can I ask you something?' I said.

'Fire away,' said Scott.

'That letter you sent.'

'I was drunk, Jo-Jo. I've told you this already.'

'I know, but some of the things you said.'

He stopped walking and turned me towards him. 'I meant all of it,' he said.

'But I'm married. I have a child. You know I'm not going to walk away from that.'

'You don't have to. Being with me doesn't mean being without Amy.'

'It means Amy not having a proper family, being without her dad. I can't do that to her.'

He looked down at the sand.

'Can't we just have some fun?' I said.

He shrugged. 'Is that all you want?'

'It's all I can have, Scott.'

'It makes me feel a bit used.'

I laughed. 'Used. You didn't seem too bothered by that this morning.'

'I'm serious, Jo-Jo. I was hoping for more.'

I met his eyes. It felt as though a full stop had been jabbed in place. I looked at the horizon. The sea had reappeared. 'Tide's coming in,' I said.

*

'Dear Jo-Jo,

I guess this was always going to be the way our relationship ended. I will never forget how good you've made me feel, how much I've enjoyed your company, and how empty I feel knowing that we're over.

It has been worthwhile, you know. Call it fate if you want, but it was like a drug and we became addicted. No-one, nothing can erase all of our wonderful memories and, even though the feelings will fade in time in order for each of us to survive, you'll never truly leave me. Walking on the beach with you, your laughter when we got lost and had to go round and round those traffic islands – 'Let's go round one more time for the hell of it' – playing Chris de Burgh's 'Diamond in the Dark' down the telephone, tomato juice and plain crisps, that cowboy hat you wore for Chester Zoo, getting drunk in Oxford and not being able to drive home until the next day, driving naked down those country lanes when those blokes caught us making love, our wonderful field, our picnics in the park...and on and on the list goes.

I love you, but it's not enough and it's not to be. You have to face up to the realities of life, your daughter needs you, your guilt is wearing you down, and I need to sort out my life without you. I feel so lost at the moment. I need to be guided through this dark tunnel, but, sadly, I feel as though I've lost my guide. We shouldn't underestimate the importance of what has happened here. Life can be such a lonely existence, but sometimes you meet someone and it all makes sense. If only we'd met at another time.

Take care of yourself for me and be happy.

All my love

Your crazy man Xxx x'

'Dear Jo-Jo,

Scott's 'Dear John' arrived today, the one you've been expecting since Cleethorpes.

He's right when he says it was always going to end this way. You've always been honest with him, but he thought if he kept saying what he wanted it would come true, like unicorns or fairies. But everyone has to grow up sometime and he heard the clang of certainty in your voice on the beach.

You'll be fine. That's the word. Fine. You'll be fine on your own. That's a truth you slammed in place years ago. You'll concentrate on Amy, that's the right thing to do, and try to ignore the mood sucking misery of your marriage. It wasn't as though Scott was the one, your soul mate, but you'll miss the warmth, the way he looked at you, the way he wanted you, the way he cuddled you. You'll be fine though. You'll suffocate the emotion, bury it so deep even you can't find the key. That's what you do.

Scott's going to be fine as well. You'll see him at a train station five years from now, he'll smile at you from the opposite platform, you'll put up your hand, but he'll have already turned away and walked back to a woman sitting on a bench with a toddler at her side. The little girl will jump on his lap, the woman will lean over and kiss him on the cheek. He'll have found a new story, and you'll walk off the platform in search of a coffee. No-one will notice you're late home. Amy will be at school. Jason will be in his study.

Everyone will be fine.

Take care of yourself.

All my love.

Jo-Jo xxx'

Me and Freddie were lying on my bed, underneath my *Starsky and Hutch Gran Torino* poster. Freddie was turning a 'Love Is' statue over in his hand, a naked boy and girl kissing. The inscription on the base read, 'Love is being together...or being with you.' 'Who gave you this?' he said.

'It's not mine. It's Josh's. Some girl in the year below him left it on his desk. It's cute.'

'It's vomit inducing.'

I held out my hand. 'Hand it over, Philistine. You have no soul.'

'I have class,' he said, handing me the statue. 'That's why I chose you.'

'Oh, you chose me. I seem to remember it was me that asked you to dance.'

'Yeah, well, I'd have got there eventually.'

'So you say. I think I'd still be waiting, waiting for Christmas.'

'Talking of Christmas...'

'We've already had this conversation, Freddie. I can't organise your Christmas afternoon. What's your mum going to say?'

'She's never bothered, not since Dad died. She cooks the dinner and goes to bed early. It's a bad day for her.'

'Mine's not much better,' I said. 'Dad tries his best, but Mum's a bit, well, you know, and Josh stays in his room, playing his Genesis albums.'

'So let's do something at mine. Even if it's just you and me.'

I looked down at the statue. 'Are you sure your mum will be okay about it?'

'She'll be glad. She might even stay up for a bit.'

'You need to ask her, see what she says.'

'I've already asked her. She's fine with it.'

I looked again at the statue. 'Okay, but we'll keep it simple. Wine. We'll have wine, Merlot, everyone likes Merlot, and trifle, the Bird's Eye one, covered in hundreds and thousands sprinkles. What about the tree?'

'We don't normally bother?'

'You can't have Christmas without a tree, Freddie. Come on.'

'Where are we going?'

'To get a tree.'

'They do some cheap ones in Woolworths.'

'There's no way we're having artificial. That Greengrocer in Bloxwich is selling real ones.'

*

We dragged the seven foot Christmas tree one and a half miles from the Greengrocer's, through the slush of melted snow, and back to Freddie's house. His mum was looking out of the bay window, waiting for us. She opened the front door. 'It's huge,' she said. 'Where are we going to put it?'

'I thought we'd put it in the front room,' said Freddie.

She looked at the tree and then at me. 'Is that what you'd do?' she said.

'No. I'd put it in the room you sit in the most.'

'But that's the dining room,' said Freddie. 'It's nowhere near big enough.'

'It is if we move the sideboard,' said his mum. 'Come on. You'll need a pot to put it in.'

Freddie followed her through the white driveway gates. I sat down on the doorstep, thinking I'd get chance for a breather, but they returned minutes later. Freddie was carrying a turquoise ceramic plant pot, which had gold stars around its centre and handles on each side. 'Will this do?' he said.

'Course it will,' said his mum.

'It's wonderful,' I said.

'Now,' said his mum. 'I've got some decorations out of the loft. We haven't used them for years.'

'We've bought some…'

'That's great,' I said, cutting across Freddie's sentence. 'Did you bring a shovel, Freddie?'

'What for?' he said.

'You need to fill the pot with dirt.'

'You can get some from there,' said his mum, nodding towards the border under the privet hedge.

Freddie walked off again through the white gates.

His mum laughed. 'Looks like he's met his match,' she said.

*

We waited while Freddie's mum cleared the ornaments from the top of the oak-veneered sideboard. Most of them she carried into the kitchen and stood on the pine work surface, but she clutched the pink dish with a dancing nymph statue as its centre piece. 'His dad bought it me,' she said when she saw me looking. 'He was drunk when he bought it, but I've had it a long time.' With the top cleared, me and Freddie moved the sideboard about three foot along the wall. 'There,' said his mum. 'You can put your tree in there. I'll wait until you've finished before putting the ornaments back.' She looked at Freddie. 'I know how clumsy you are.'

We'd left the tree, now planted in the ceramic pot, in the hallway. We stood each side of it. I couldn't see Freddie because the tree was in the way. One of the branches was brushing against my face. I could smell the pine needles, some of them had already shed into the dirt. 'We'll have to water this,' I said. 'But let's get it in place first.'

'Are you walking backwards or shall I?' said Freddie.

'Definitely you,' I said.

'We haven't got much lift leeway,' he said.

I looked up. There was only about four inches between the top of the tree and the artex of the hallway ceiling. 'We've got enough,' I said, grabbing the handle. With a grunt from both of us we lifted the tree off the floor, the top brushing against the ceiling. 'Drop it down a touch,' I said. 'Okay. Ready. Walk.'

We shuffled along the hallway, me nervously watching the ceiling.

'Waddle, waddle, waddle, waddle.'

'What are you doing?'

'Keeping myself motivated. Waddle, waddle, waddle, waddle...'

We carried on shuffling, Freddie carried on with his waddle chant.

'Waddle, waddle, waddle, waddle.'

I laughed. He laughed.

'You're nearly there,' said his mum.

I felt my cheeks flush. I'd forgotten she was watching.

*

We were sitting on the floor unravelling tinsel. Freddie's mum was sitting in the rocking chair, pulling decorations, one by one, out of a brown hessian sack, which had Freddie's name embroidered across the front in red cotton. 'He's had that since he was born,' she said. 'His Aunt Floss made it for him.' The champions of the bag were dusty 1950s baubles, mainly gold and blue, and a set of ten hand-carved wooden soldiers dressed in red uniforms and wearing foreign legion hats, which looked like fezzes but with a veil down the back and a wide-rimmed peak. 'I can't remember where we got those from,' said his mum, holding up one of the models.

'Aunt Jess,' said Freddie. 'She gave them to us after Dad died.'

'Oh yes,' said his mum.

'That was Dad's sister,' Freddie said to me.

'Still is,' said his mum. 'But we've not seen her since the funeral.'

They exchanged glances, making me feel like I was intruding

on some dark family secret. 'Anyway,' said his mum. 'I'll make some tea. Put some music on, Freddie.'

'Music,' he said.

'Yes. That old record player still works. Pop that Abba album on you bought. I like them.' She walked into the kitchen and we could hear her filling the kettle and humming 'Dancing Queen'.

'I don't know what you've done to her,' said Freddie. 'She never wants the record player on.'

He stood up, walked over to the Ferguson cabinet record player, selected the Abba *Arrival* LP out of the storage rack, a picture of the band in a helicopter on the front cover, and pulled the record out of its sleeve. He dropped the black vinyl onto the turntable, lifted up the stylus arm, which triggered the turntable to start revolving, and placed the needle on the far edge of the record. The crackling sound of 'When I Kissed the Teacher' started up through the single built in speaker. 'Turn it up,' shouted his mum. ' I can hardly hear it.'

Freddie did as he was told and sat down next to me on the floor. 'This is all your fault,' he said, kissing me.

'Me. What have I done?'

'Being so gorgeous. She clearly likes you.'

His mum came back into the room, carrying a silver tray loaded with a teapot, three cups and saucers, a milk jug and a sugar bowl. Freddie jumped up and grabbed the tray. 'You should have called me,' he said.

'I'm quite capable of carrying a tray,' she said. 'Put it down on the table and I'll pour. You two can start putting the decorations on the tree.'

'We need to get it the right way first,' I said.

'What do you mean?' said Freddie, still holding the tray.

'I mean we need to turn it to different positions, see what looks best.'

'It's a tree, Jo-Jo.'

'You just do the turning, Freddie. Your mum and I will tell when it's right.'

'Best put the tray down and listen to her, son,' said his mum. 'She knows what she's doing.'

*

Christmas Day – me, Freddie and his mum settled down for dinner, which we ate on our laps in front of the Christmas tree. His mum had cooked roast beef, home-made Yorkshire pudding, sprouts, cabbage and mashed potatoes, all smothered in gravy that made my mouth salivate to bursting point. 'This gravy is delicious,' I said.

'Perhaps I'll show you how to make it,' she said.

I smiled and looked at the tree. We'd wound his mum's pink and white candle lights around its branches, used hardly any tinsel and placed a peg fairy in a white ballerina dress on the tree's summit. At the bottom of the tree, there were four wrapped presents, one from me and Freddie to each other, one from us to his mum, and, most intriguing of all, one from Freddie's mum to us. 'What's she bought us?' I said when I saw it under the tree.

'I have no idea,' he said. 'But it's making me very nervous.' On a small coffee table next to the tree, his mum had placed a wooden model of a church with a red roof, which was lit up. Before we started our meal, she wound up the key on the back of the church and it played 'O Little Town of Bethlehem.'

'It's beautiful,' I said.

'It was his dad's,' she said.

Once we'd finished dinner, Freddie stacked up the plates from the table and disappeared into the kitchen. His mum rolled her eyes. 'He's been waiting to deliver this all day. Men. They always make a mountain out of a trifle.' I laughed as Freddie came back into the room, carrying a glass dish as though he were serving it to a Maharaja's banquet.

'Tada,' he said, laying the dish in the centre of the table. 'The pièce de résistance.'

'Freddie,' said his mum, 'it's a trifle.'

'No,' he said, sitting down. 'It's a trifle made by me.'

'We'll need some dishes if we're going to enjoy your great work.'

'Oh yeah,' he said, going to stand back up.

'Stay there,' she said. 'I'll get them.'

She rubbed the top of his head before walking off into the kitchen. Freddie beamed after her.

'She's lovely,' I said.

'You're good for her,' he said, squeezing my hand. 'Was your dad okay with you coming here today?'

'He seemed to be. Mum's in bed and Josh has gone to his mates.'

'So your dad's on his own. He could have joined us.'

'He can't. He needs to stay with mum.'

'It must be lonely for him with the way your mum is.'

I felt an itch of irritation creep under my skin. Dad's woman in the park dropped into my head. 'That's what being married means, isn't it? Better or worse.'

'I suppose so. I just meant you've got to admire him. The way he...'

'He's not a Saint, Freddie.'

He put his hand on top of mine. 'I didn't say he was. Are you okay?'

'Yeah, sorry, it's, well, me and Dad don't get on these days.'

His mum walked back into the room, holding three pudding dishes and three spoons, which she set out in front of us. 'What are you two looking so serious about?' she said.

'Oh, nothing,' said Freddie. 'I was just telling Jo-Jo about the secret ingredient in the trifle.'

'Secret ingredient?' she said.

'Navy rum,' he said. 'I slopped a couple of glasses in with the jelly.'

I was conscious all the way through eating my trifle of the unfinished conversation. Side one of the Abba album finished with 'Knowing Me, Knowing You' and Freddie stood up, walked over to the music system and turned the record over. Side two started up with 'Money, Money, Money'.

'Well, I have to say, for a packet trifle, that was delicious,' said his mum, placing her spoon back in her now empty dish.

'It was lovely, Freddie,' I said.

'Shall we open the presents?' his mum said.

Me and Freddie looked at each other.

'Do you want to open my present first?' she said.

Freddie grabbed it from under the tree and handed it to me like it was a live grenade.

'It's okay,' she said. 'It won't bite.'

I looked at the card and showed it to Freddie. 'May these keep you safe, wherever life takes you. xx'

'What is it?' said Freddie.

'Well, if you open it, you'll find out.'

I started to unpick the wrapping paper. I could feel straightaway there were two ring boxes inside. I looked at Freddie's mum.

'What?' she said.

A lump wedged in my throat at the thought of what she might have bought, what she might have assumed. We'd only been together a matter of weeks. I pulled the red velvet boxes free of the wrapping.

Freddie looked horrified. 'Mum,' he said. 'What…'

'The pair of you needn't look so worried,' she said. 'Open the boxes.'

I opened the lid on the first box and smiled. 'A St Christopher,' I said.

'There are name labels in the lid,' she said.

I looked. The label in the box I'd opened said Freddie. I handed it to him and opened the second box. A matching St Christopher, gold, about the size of a sixpence.

'I've guessed the length of the chains,' she said.

I undid the clasp, put the chain around my neck and fastened it. The medallion sat just below my collarbone. 'It's perfect,' I said. Freddie put his on. 'They're wonderful, Mum,' he said.

I hugged her. 'Thank you. I'll keep it with me always.'

*

Me and Freddie washed up, him washing, me drying, while his mum snoozed in the rocking chair. She'd protested about us doing it, but only half-heartedly.

'Do you want to tell me about your dad?' said Freddie as he washed the meat dish.

'He had an affair,' I said, not looking at him, concentrating on drying the plates. I waited for a few seconds for him to say something, but then realised I might have said it too sharply, as though it was none of his business. 'It's nice to be able to tell someone,' I said.

'Who was she?'

'Some woman he used to meet in the park. I saw him on a bench with her.'

He stopped washing up, dried his hands and hugged me. 'That must have been awful.'

'Yes,' I said. 'It was.'

'Does your mum know?'

'Dad never told her, and I've never had the guts.'

'He stayed though.'

'He said he loves Mum, but I think he just feels sorry for her.'

'I think he loves her from what I've seen.'

'What he did with his tart wasn't love.'

'No,' he said, turning back to the sink.

I rubbed his back. 'Let's not talk about it anymore. I don't want Dad spoiling our day. Do you think your mum will have a drink with us?'

'No idea. She's a different woman round you.'

'Let's go and ask her then.'

His mum opened her eyes when we walked in from the kitchen. 'What have you got there?' she said to Freddie, who was carrying a bottle of Pernod and a bottle of Crème-de-Menthe, which he put down on the dining table. 'We thought we'd have a drink, Mum.'

'Unless you want Advocaat,' I said. 'We've bought some soda water and lime juice so I can make snowballs if you like.'

She sat up in the rocking chair. 'Isn't that an old woman's drink?'

'You like Advocaat, Mum.'

'I'll have what you're having,' she said, looking at the bottles.

Freddie shrugged and fetched three whisky glasses out of the sideboard. I opened the Crème-de-Menthe, splashed a measure in each glass and then put in double the amount of Pernod. I handed Freddie's mum one of the glasses, picked up one myself and Freddie picked up the third. 'Happy Christmas,' said Freddie, holding his glass out in front of him. We clinked our glasses together and took a sip.

'It tastes like the gob-smackers we used to have as kids,' Freddie's mum said, curling her legs underneath her and taking another sip. 'It gets nicer the more you drink.'

'We get through a fair few in Max's,' I said. 'Be careful though. They say Pernod makes you drunk from the legs upwards.'

'Time for *Top of the Pops*,' said Freddie, switching on the television and flopping down next to me on the two seater settee. He squeezed my hand, the theme music to *Top of the Pops* started up, Peter Powell and Kid Jensen appeared on screen. 'You don't have to watch this, Mum.'

'Oh, I like him,' she said. 'Don't they call the other one 'Puffter' Powell?'

'Mother.'

'Everyone says he looks gay,' I said.

'That's it,' said his mum.

Boney M opened the show with 'Mary's Boy Child', the band dressed in white fur coats with hoods, B.A. Robertson did 'Bang Bang', Legs and Co danced to Anita Ward's 'Ring My Bell' and Blondie did two songs, Debbie Harry dressed in her Parallel Lines dress, sunglasses on for 'Sunday Girl' and off for 'Dreaming'. 'That's our song,' I said when 'Dreaming' started up. 'I asked him to dance when that song was on.'

'You asked him to dance?'

'She beat me to it by seconds,' said Freddie, putting his arm around me.

'You never were very quick off the mark,' she said, without taking her eyes off the television. 'Me and his dad had the Beatles.'

'Really,' I said. 'My dad loves them. What's your favourite?'

"All My Loving," she said, emptying her glass and looking at Freddie. 'I don't think I've ever told you that.'

'No, but it's nice to hear you talk about Dad.'

'These are all miming,' she said, looking back at the television. 'I think they have to,' I said.

'I'd like to have seen them tell John Lennon that. Are we going to have another drink?'

Freddie's Dad

I've spent a lot of time over the years wondering what it would have been like if Dad hadn't died so young, what our relationship might have been, good, bad, indifferent, how it could have changed me as a person. When he died, I made up a story about him being locked in a room somewhere, fast asleep on the springs of a steel framed single bed, waking up, asking for us, but no-one knew where we were. I imagined how he looked, perhaps he'd grown a beard, maybe he looked like a bedraggled shipwrecked sailor, Robinson Crusoe. Some mornings I'd run downstairs expecting him to be there. I used to stand in the garden talking to him, looking up at the clouds or the stars, convinced he could hear me, picking out a star, asking him if he was okay. Mum thought I was too young to go to his funeral. I was sent off to stay with Miss Reece, two doors down, a Mrs Danvers character, who made me sit quietly and read. Dead, funeral, the words meant nothing. One minute Dad was home and I was lying in bed with him while he sang 'Maggie May' – and the next he was gone.

Freddie – December 1979

I cuddled Jo-Jo into my chest and we knotted our bodies together on the two seater sofa. *Top of the Pops* had finished, we'd turned off the telly and Mum had gone to have a lie down. 'I'll be back for the *Poseidon Adventure* though,' she'd said as she left the room. 'And if you make a cup of tea, bring me one up.'

'You're quiet,' said Jo-Jo, pinching my arm.

'I was thinking about my dad,' I said.

She lifted her head and looked at me. 'You don't talk about him much,' she said.

'Not much to say. I don't really remember him.'

'If you ever do need to talk, I'm a good listener.'

'I know. I'm glad you came round today. You're good with her. I've never seen her like that. It's usually all doom and gloom.'

'Well, she has had a tough life. It can't have been easy, him dying so young.'

I kissed the top of her head. 'How did you get so wise?'

She kissed me on the lips. 'Shall we have another drink?'

'We could, but I've suddenly got a very urgent urge.'

'Really,' she said, smiling. 'And what urge would that be?'

'Oh, I think you know. And it's probably a life or death scenario.'

'Your mum's upstairs.'

'She won't come down.'

'Okay,' she said, pulling me towards her. 'If it's life or death, we'd better see if we can sort this urge of yours.'

*

We ended up on our backs, lying side by side on the carpet, looking up at the ceiling, the cushions off the sofa scattered around us. 'Jesus,' I said.

'My thoughts exactly. That was quite an urge you had.' She turned over and dropped her head on my chest. 'Your heart's racing.'

'I'm not surprised. Do you think Mum heard anything?'

'She might have heard that whimper you do.'

'I don't whimper. When?'

'Just before, you know, it's cute, but it's quite loud.'

I sat up and looked at her. 'I whimper?'

'Sort of, like you're clearing your throat, but a bit higher pitched. Don't you know you're doing it?'

'If I was going to choose a noise, it would be something a bit more manly than a whimper.'

'Like what?'

'I don't know, a roar maybe.'

'Go on then. Let's hear it.'

I roared three times.

'I prefer the whimper. And you only do it once.'

'Oh, that's okay then. You're enjoying this aren't you?'

She whimpered.

'Stop it,' I said, kissing her lips.

She whimpered again, this time muffled and into my mouth.

'You are completely bonkers.'

'And you, Mister, have got to make your mum a cup of tea.'

'I can't go up there. What am I going to say to her?'

'You should have thought about that when you had your urge.'

*

I made the tea, left Jo-Jo tidying the room, and walked upstairs and into Mum's bedroom. She was lying on top of the duvet, fast asleep, still wearing her moccasin slippers. The curtains were half closed, putting the room in semi-darkness. I placed the tea on her bedside cabinet, next to the wooden cottage jewellery box I'd bought her two Christmases ago. 'Mum,' I said. 'I've brought your tea.'

'Freddie,' she said, opening her eyes.

I sat down on the side of the bed and held her hand.

'I was fast asleep,' she said. 'It must be that drink you gave me.' She sat up and reached for the cup and saucer.

I picked it up for her and put it into her hands.

'That's nice,' she said, taking a sip.

'The St Christophers are lovely, Mum.'

'Does Jo-Jo like hers?'

'She loves it. She's put it on already.'

'She's a nice girl. You really like her, don't you?'

'She's perfect, Mum.'

'Then make sure you don't lose her. Take it from me, perfect doesn't happen that often.'

'Dad was perfect, wasn't he?'

'He had his moments, but I never wanted anyone else from the day I met him. Why are you asking?'

'I was thinking about him. I don't really remember him.'

'I can see him in you.'

'I'm not perfect.'

She took another sip of her tea. 'You're perfect enough. You just need to realise it. Now, let me drink my tea in peace and I'll come down and watch that film with you.'

I stood up and walked towards the door.

'Freddie,' she said.

I turned back towards her.

'You could have closed the lounge door, you know.'

Freddie – August 2015

Over the years, Jack had a plethora of short-term tenants living in the house next door. None of them stayed very long, but we gave them all nicknames and watched from a distance as they played out their colourful lives:

Lorry Driver and Grey Beard – Lorry Driver would go away for days on end, but within half an hour of him pulling off his drive, Grey Beard, his best mate, would turn up in a Mini Metro, go into the house and the next thing we'd hear through the walls was creaking bed springs, a rattling headboard and groans of 'Yes, yes, yes' from Mrs Lorry Driver. When her husband returned three days later, Grey Beard would turn up again, this time with his partner, an older woman who wore gold bracelets on each wrist and hooped earrings. The two couples would sit in the back garden, laughing and drinking beer as though everything was fine with the world.

Six Foot Blondie and Stumpy Short-Arse – Blondie used to clean her BMW sports car wearing a bosom squeezing white cotton t-shirt and buttock revealing frayed denim shorts; her ex-husband, also blond, also six-foot, was always at the house she shared with Stumpy. One day, Stumpy fell off his motorbike at the end of the cul-de-sac and ex-husband helped him limp down the drive, one gentle step at a time, Blondie watching and laughing from the back gate. Eventually, Stumpy was left on his own with the budgie. 'Just you and me now, mate,' we heard him say through the walls.

Anthony and Cleopatra – Cleopatra used to attend the village hairdresser's twice a week, not a split end in sight, and her nails, Jack couldn't help noticing, were filed, shaped and painted to perfection. Anthony spent most of his time outside in his dirty blue overalls, cutting the grass, weeding and digging the borders, smoking his cigarettes at the top of the drive. We assumed he'd been barred from the house, that Cleopatra made him sit on a *Guardian* newspaper when he went indoors for meals. They doted on their daughter, an only child, and obsessed about their rabbit, which regularly escaped through the fence into Jack's garden. Cleopatra would knock on Jack's door and they'd go out looking under bushes in a desperate search, shouting 'Mopsy' at the top of their voices. The bunny would always be found, usually chewing on a dandelion leaf, and be whisked away with a guilty look and twitching nostrils.

The Brothers – The older one, a chef, used to shout, 'I'm off down the nags,' before driving his battered white transit van to the pub, driving it back at midnight, drunk, parking it diagonally and two foot away from the kerb, going into the house, slamming the front door and pissing a waterfall into the toilet. One day Chef hung his freshly washed whites on a nail he'd banged into Jack's new fence. Jack went round, knocked on the door, younger brother answered and told Jack to pull the nail out, which Jack did. The whites lay on the grass for about a week.

Barney Boombox – He had a voice that reverberated through the street foundations, bounced off the walls and landed with an sonic-boom inside your head. One day, we saw him in Currys buying a surround sound system, which, when he fitted it to his speakerphone, amplified any callers' voices to match Boombox's.

He used to set his alarm to the Today programme on Radio 4, which would wake Jack at six o'clock every morning on the dot. The only time he was quiet was when his girlfriend visited every few weeks and the whole house would fall into graveyard silence – Jack swore she unplugged his speakers when she first arrived and made him whisper as a condition of her staying. One day, Jack went round to his house to complain about the noise and came back with a recipe for curried goat.

Jo-Jo – August 1980

Me and Freddie kissed our goodbye outside the chip shop in Bloxwich, him having walked the twenty minutes journey from his house to mine so we could catch the bus together. We'd already been into Woolworths to get my quarter pound of liquorice comforts to help get me through the shift. 'Last day,' I said. 'I can't wait to get away from that cow.'

'And I get you to myself on a Saturday.'

'Until I go to uni. I can't believe that's only weeks away.'

'I'm still hoping you might change your mind.'

'I'm not going to change my mind, Freddie. We've talked this to death.'

He dropped his gaze into the gutter. I lifted his head. 'What are you going to do with yourself today?'

'Wait for you to finish work.'

'Can't you go to Jack's?'

'He's studying. I'll be fine. I'll get some breakfast at the greasy spoon and then crash out in King George's.'

'Sounds better than my day.'

'It'll go by in a flash,' he said.

I kissed him lightly on the lips, squeezed his hand and then walked away along the high street, leaving him outside the chip shop. I could feel him watching me, making sure I was okay. I smiled to myself. Sweet.

I reached the M.E.B, turned and waved. He waved back. I looked down the alleyway at the side of the shop. There were three overflowing grey metal bins in front of me, a mound of used tealeaves spilling out of the first bin, its lid plonked precariously on a heap of rubbish. The stench of rotting fruit and food waste invaded my nostrils as I walked, trying to hold my breath, to the fire escape stairs halfway down the alley. I climbed the rackety metal steps, feeling them swaying underneath me, and opened the door to the hairdressers, which occupied the top floor.

Roma was sitting in one of the black leather barber's chairs, facing the mirror, drinking a mug of coffee. 'You're late,' she said as I walked through the door.

'The bus was late,' I said.

She placed her coffee cup on the floor, leaned forward to look in the mirror and started pinching and stretching the skin at the side of her eyes. 'Do you think I'm getting wrinkles?'

I stood behind her, looking over her head at her face in the mirror. 'No,' I said.

'Liar.'

'I'm not lying.'

'It'll come to you one day,' she said, still looking in the mirror, still pulling at the skin on her face. 'Look at these hands. You see that, there. I swear that wasn't there last week.' I looked at the spot on the back of her right hand, which she was jabbing with her left forefinger. There was a faint brown stain about the size of a half-pence piece. 'It's there, isn't it?' she said.

'I can't see anything.'

'Age spots. My mother had them all over her body. They give you away. Especially on your hands. You'll find out.' She sighed, stood up and walked over to the small kitchenette at the back of the shop. She opened one of the cupboard doors over the sink and looked inside. 'I could have sworn we had some biscuits. That Rob's probably nicked them.'

'Nicked what?' said Rob, walking into the shop.

'Biscuits,' I said, raising my eyebrows.

'Just what she needs with that gut,' he said.

'What?' said Roma, still looking in the cupboard.

'I said I'll pop out and get some later,' said Rob, winking at me.

'Oh, you're here,' she said, turning to face us.

'Charming,' he said, pulling at the blond highlights in his feather-cut hair. 'I can always go again if you want.'

'You know she's going today, don't you?'

'I don't blame her, the way you talk to her.'

'She's a Saturday girl. That's what they're for.'

'I'll get the biscuits,' I said.

'No,' said Roma. 'You can sweep the floor. You're already late. I need some fresh air.' She walked out of the shop. We heard her heels clattering as she descended the steps .

'By fresh air she means a fag,' said Rob. 'She needs fresh everything.'

'I shan't miss her,' I said. 'She's never liked me.'

'It doesn't help you being so gorgeous. You still seeing that Freddie bloke?'

'Yes,' I said, feeling my cheeks flush. 'He's meeting me later. You're not going to stay here, are you?'

'What, with old iron-drawers? What would she do without me? Better the devil you know, I guess.'

'She needs a man,' I said.

'Maybe not say that to her,' said Rob, hanging up his coat. 'I know it's your last day, but I'm assuming you don't want to spend it in casualty.'

'Don't worry. I asked her once and nearly lost my head. You've never told me what happened with her husband.'

'Usual story. He dumped her for a younger model. I know it nearly finished her off.'

'And she never had anyone else. That must have been years ago.'

'Some things you never get over. He was a shit, but she loved him.'

'I hadn't realised,' I said, sadness suddenly smothering me like an old grey overcoat.

'Why would you? They were kids when they met, about your age. She thought they both wanted to change the world, went off to a Kibbutz in Israel, but it turned out he wanted to let her do all the work while he spent their money on booze and slept it off on the beach.'

'And she still married him?'

'Yep. Kidded herself she could change him. They dragged on for ten years, broken promise after broken promise, until the money had gone and he pissed off, leaving her with the debt. He still lives round here, turned up at the shop about five years ago, drunk, broke, on his own, begging her to take him back. I had to call the police.'

'Jesus. No wonder she's bitter.'

'Lesson for us all,' he said, grinning at me. 'Be careful of young love. It's not always what it seems.'

I heard Roma's heels coming back up the stairs.

'Better get sweeping,' said Rob.

*

Late afternoon, Rob had finished his shift, the blue rinse brigade had all been sated, and I was sweeping up the last of the, mainly grey, strands of hair. 'You'll be wanting this,' said Roma, opening the till, lifting the spring on one of the drawers and pulling out a brown pay packet. 'Not that you deserve it.'

I stopped sweeping, stood the brush against the wall and took the envelope from her. It had Jo-Jo written in capital letters across the front in red ink. 'Thank you,' I said.

'You think I'm a cow, don't you?'

'It doesn't really matter now,' I said.

She laughed. 'I don't suppose it does,' she said, closing the till drawer.

I folded up the envelope and pushed it inside my skirt pocket. 'You never seemed to like me very much. I'm not sure what I did.'

'You didn't do anything,' she said, flicking through the pages in the appointments book. 'You shouldn't be so touchy.'

I walked to the top of the stairs. I could feel her watching me, could sense that she was going to say something.

'Jo-Jo,' she said.

I stopped walking and turned back towards her.

'Do you need a reference?'

'No thanks. I'm off to uni in a couple of weeks.'

'Let me know if you do.'

'Can I ask you something?' I said.

'That depends what it is.'

'I was just, tell me to mind my own business, but, well, I've never heard you mention your family.'

'That's because I don't have any.'

'What, no one?'

'I have a sister, but she lives back in Liverpool. We don't get on.'

'And there's no one else?'

'You mean a man?'

'You're right, it's none of my business. I'm just being a nosy cow.' I went to walk down the stairs.

'Hang on,' she said, closing the appointments book and walking from behind the till. 'This young man of yours.'

'Freddie,' I said. 'What about him?'

'You love him, don't you?'

'I think so. Why are you asking?'

'I don't know really. It's just, don't let him become everything. If he loves you, he'll understand.'

'He does understand,' I said. 'That's why I'm going to uni.'

I watched her as she walked down the high street, her blue denim mini-skirt and white cheesecloth top showing off her tanned skin. She reached the alleyway, turned and waved. I waved back. She walked out of view and I stood, confusion knotting my stomach, looking at the space she'd vacated. This was what it would be like without her. I'd be left with her ghost and, even worse, three years of futile hope that she'd come back to me – a death of a thousand cuts. From that first dance in Max's, I knew she was out of my league. I still didn't get why she'd asked me to dance, why she'd stayed with me for nearly a year.

A bus screeched to a stop outside the chip shop, passengers chattering as they disembarked, jolting me out of my head space. I shoved my hands inside the pockets of my jeans and walked down the Stafford Road, heading for the park. I missed the Avenger, not because of the walk, but because it meant I wouldn't be able to park up in King George's, lie on the grass with the door open and listen to Springsteen tapes. It was okay though. I needed to save the petrol if we were going to New Invention later to play darts with Jo-Jo's cousins.

I reached the gates of the park and walked along the driveway towards the open fields. It was only ten o'clock, but I could already smell the burned charcoal of the local neighbourhood's barbeques, a sticky haze smothering the landscape like a honey and mustard dressing. The park was deserted. Normally there was a football match being played, but I remembered it was a break in season. I turned right at the top of the drive and headed up the hill towards the deserted cottage, the one Jack had convinced me was haunted. 'Seriously, Freddie. It belongs to a bloke whose bride-to-be dumped him on their wedding day. He's probably still hanging in there.' The dirty white building was hidden from view by wild bramble bushes and feral roses. Its windows had been boarded up recently by the council, but for years it had sat with broken panes of glass, shivering cobwebs hanging out of every orifice. I lay down on the grass in front of the bushes and looked up at the sky. If Jo-Jo had been there we'd have been looking at the clouds, the sun drawing out her nose freckles as we searched the heavens for famous faces.

'Freddie.'

I lifted myself up onto my elbows. Nicki was walking towards me, her pet dachshund, Sacha, trotting on a lead at her side. I put up my hand, hoping she'd walk straight past, but she walked over, unclipped the dog's lead so he could sniff along the bushes and then sat down beside me on the grass. 'You okay,' she said. 'Still with, what's her name?'

'Jo-Jo,' I said. 'And yes, we're still together. What about you? Still with…'

'Tommy,' she said. 'No. We called it a day. I couldn't cope with all that navy rubbish.'

I smiled.

'No need to look so pleased,' she said.

'You did dump me for him. I never understood what you saw in a bugle player from the sea cadets.'

'Hey, he's an excellent bugle player. He can play 'Reveille' all the way through.'

'I wouldn't have thought there was much call for that in Walsall. We've all got alarm clocks.'

She laughed. 'You're probably right. Anyway, I did you a favour from what I can hear.'

'And what have you heard?'

'That she's gorgeous, that you're inseparable, that you look at her with puppy dog eyes.'

I felt the blood fill my cheeks.

'Oh God,' she said. 'It's true. Freddie's in love.'

I looked around at the bushes. Sacha had found himself a stick to gnaw on. 'You've still got the dog then?'

'Stop changing the subject. I'm pleased. You deserve someone to look after you.'

'She's off to uni soon.'

'Brains as well as beauty. What does she see in you?'

'My thoughts exactly.'

She gave me a hard look. 'I was joking, Freddie. You're not overthinking this are you? You know what you're like.'

'I was right about you and the bugle player.'

'That was my mistake, not yours.'

'It still happened though.'

Sacha came bounding over and nudged at Nicki's elbow. 'Listen, I've got to go,' she said, patting my leg. 'But call me if you need to talk.'

'Thanks,' I said. 'I will.'

'There is one thing this Jo-Jo can't claim,' she said, standing up and reattaching Sacha's lead.

I gave her a puzzled look.

'Your virginity. That was me on my mum's sheepskin rug. Don't tell me you've forgotten.'

'I haven't forgotten,' I said. 'It's a pity I couldn't play the bugle. We could have played reveille afterwards.'

She laughed and walked away towards the entrance gates, Sacha's stunted legs sprinting hard to keep up.

Jo-Jo – August 2015

I lost my virginity on Macfisheries' car park in the passenger seat of an MGBGT. I was sixteen. His name was Micky Kumar. Five years older than me, a Hindu, born in India and raised in Bilston, his mum came from Begur village on the outskirts of Bangalore. She followed his dad to this country in the early sixties and worked as a typist for West Midlands Police. Micky used to tell me stories about the racism. 'It's not like they try and cover it up. There's a powerlifter and an ex-marine who drive around in the fast response car trying to nick their daily 'paki' quota. They're saying this in front of her, like she's invisible.' Micky dumped me the day after the MGBGT fumble.

'So you've had your fun and now you're running.'

'Lighten up, Jo-Jo. Mum and Dad want me to marry a nice Indian girl. They've already sorted me a list of possibilities.'

'A list?'

'Yeah, that's the way we do things. It's better than meeting some random bloke in a bar.'

It felt like I was his revenge shag. Joe Jackson's song 'Is She Really Going Out With Him?' came out later in the year. It was about a man people watching from his apartment, pointing out how all the women in his neighbourhood were dating 'gorillas'. Me and Karen interpreted the lyrics as being about black men dating white women. 'You're best rid,' said Karen.

'It just seems so pointless,' I said. The last I heard of Micky, he'd married a British Airways Hostess from Milton Keynes. She was white and he met her in a nightclub.

Freddie – May 1980

Blackpool. Early morning. I could hear Jo-Jo breathing next to me. There was a cock crowing somewhere close, perhaps next door to Mr Lewis's B and B. The bedroom smelt of sleep and sex. A gentle breeze from the open window was cooling my face. Tap, tap, tap. Anxiety, the voice that kept me awake at night, was knocking out its rhythm inside my head. 'She's too good for you.' Turn off my brain, turn off my brain. 'You're not good enough for her.' I moved closer and eased myself against her body. She muttered something and threw her arm across me. The heat glow from her naked skin was comforting, like the afterglow of a hot chocolate drink on a zero degrees winter's day. 'She not going to stay.' Shut it out, shut it out. 'You know what's going to happen.' I cuddled her closer. She rolled over and turned her back on me. Don't go. Don't go. Don't go. The cock crowed again.

Freddie – August 2015

I could hear them talking in the hallway, but their voices were whisper level and I couldn't make out what they were saying. I tried to concentrate on Elton John's *Blue Moves*, which was playing at low volume out of the Bose sound dock, but Amy's voice was distracting me. I'd suspected she would come, but the reality of Jo-Jo and I talking in front of her ratcheted up my pulse rate and churned my stomach. I could have done with a Propranolol to settle my nerves, but that wasn't possible now. 'Of course she wants her here,' I said to myself. 'She probably thinks you're mad and she needs a chaperone.' Jack had said he'd go out, but, covering all the possibilities, he'd laid out four cups and saucers alongside the coffee percolator, milk and sugar bowl on the glass topped table in front of me. I suddenly realised he hadn't given us any teaspoons. I ticked off the mistake in my head – Jack not getting it one hundred per cent right proved he was human. I stood up, ready to go into the kitchen to fetch the spoons, but I heard the front door close. I sat back down in the Next bucket chair and waited. The lounge door opened.

'Hello, Freddie.'

I burst into tears and Jo-Jo rushed over to me. 'I'm so sorry,' I said as she hugged me to her.

She squeezed me tighter. 'So am I,' she said. 'So am I.'

*

Our hug started to feel tense after a few seconds, the initial relief ebbing away and bringing us back into the confusion of the real world. We came apart and Jo-Jo sat down on the other bucket seat and crossed her legs. I blew my nose into a paper tissue.

'Jack said you're going to stay here for a few days,' she said.

'He thought it best. I think he's worried about what I might do next.'

'You can't blame him, Freddie.'

'I know. I've messed it all up again.'

'You mustn't say that.'

'It's true though.'

A silence descended. I looked at the floor.

'I need to know why,' she said.

'I don't know. When you told me about the baby, it all seemed, I couldn't stop thinking about it and…'

'I wanted to be honest with you, Freddie. I've held that guilt inside for thirty-five years.'

I lifted my head and met her eyes. 'I should have phoned you, should have been with you. I should have, I don't know, I wish we could go back to the beginning.' I started crying again and she came over and knelt in front of me, stroking my hair.

'Everyone wants that,' she said. 'It wasn't anyone's fault. You've got to stop blaming yourself for everything.' She pulled a fresh tissue out of the Kleenex box at the side of the chair and handed it to me.

'We were good,' I said, taking the clean tissue from her and blowing my nose again.

'Yes,' she said. 'But we were kids.'

'I mean in Devon. It was still there, wasn't it? Tell me you felt it as well.'

'Of course I did.'

'Then we can make it right, can't we? Even now we can make it right.' I hugged her to me, sniffing in her white musk perfume, which always took me back to Max's and our first dance. 'Tell me it's all going to be okay,' I whispered.

Jo-Jo – August 2015

I had my hands on his shoulder blades. He felt bony. He'd lost weight in the few days since I'd last seen him and he seemed older, shrunken, the nervy Freddie from the hotel meal was back, not the Devon Freddie, certainly not the Max's Freddie, not my Freddie. He was squeezing me tight, like he was scared I'd run away if he loosened his grip. I eased myself away from him. I noticed he wasn't wearing his Ray-Ban spectacles. Crow's feet wrinkles had spread their reach from the corners of his eyes and onto his cheeks, and patches of grey beard stubble were dotted across his face and neck.

'It is going to be okay, isn't it?' he said.

'I don't know,' I said.

'You don't love me.'

'I've never stopped loving you, Freddie.'

'That's okay then. We can work all of this out.'

I started to think about Mum, her Schizophrenia, how it had smothered Dad's existence, driven him to an affair with his tart. 'It's not that simple,' I said. 'You frighten me when you react like this.'

'I'll change. You can help me change.'

'It's not about me. First the train, now the tablets. You need to get well.'

'Who told you about the train?'

'Jack. He was worried about you. What you did isn't normal.' I realised what I'd said as soon as the words tipped out of my mouth. His face crumpled. He looked like I'd punched him on the nose. 'I didn't mean that,' I said.

He stood up and walked over to the bay window. 'When do you go to New Zealand?' he said.

'Come and sit down, Freddie. Come and talk to me.'

'You should go,' he said, turning to face me. 'I'm still not sure why you came looking for me in the first place.'

I stood up, walked over to him and went to touch his face.

He turned his head away. 'Please, Jo-Jo. Leave me alone.'

'I don't want us to finish like this.'

'What do you want?' he said, his voice bubbling with emotion. 'We finished thirty-five years ago, but you decided to start it all again.'

'I know and…'

'And what? You came away to Devon knowing how I feel about you.'

'I felt the same.'

'And then you decided to tell me about the baby.'

'I thought you had a right to know. I didn't expect you to react like you did.'

'Why? You know me better than anyone. How could you not know how I'd react?'

'I thought I was doing the right thing.'

'I love you, Jo-Jo. You say you love me, but you're going to walk away.'

I went to touch his face again.

'Please go,' he said.

The lounge door opened. 'Mum,' said Amy. 'Are you okay?'

I hadn't realised, but I'd started crying. 'No,' I said. 'We need to go.' I turned and walked out of the lounge, pushing past Amy and Jack who were standing side by side in the doorway.

'What have you said to her?' said Amy.

I was still standing by the window, but I'd turned back towards the street. I saw Jo-Jo walk, half run down the garden path. She pressed her key fob and the Mazda's lights flickered twice. She opened the driver's door and got into the car. 'Nothing,' I said.

Jack walked across the lounge and put his arm around me. 'You okay, mate?' he said.

'She thinks I'm mad, Jack.'

'Well...' said Amy.

Jack glared at her and she stopped whatever it was she was going to say.

'I'm going to check Mum's okay,' she said and walked out of the lounge.

'Come on,' said Jack. 'Let's sit down.'

He guided me back to the bucket chair. I felt as though I was in a trance, being led back to my seat by Matron on the psychiatric ward.

Jack knelt in front of me. 'What's happened?' he said.

'She's going to New Zealand. She always was.'

'Is that what she said?'

'I think I've frightened her.'

'You frightened all of us, bud.'

I suddenly realised how he was talking to me, carefully, thinking about what he was saying, no sarcasm, no edge. Not Jack. 'Do you think I'm mad, Jack?'

'No,' he said. 'But you need some help. We can't ignore what's happened. What you tried to do.'

'I don't want to see her again.'

'You don't mean that.'

'I do, Jack. I can't bear the thought of her seeing me like this. Why did she come back?'

'To see you.'

'And the baby, I didn't need to know about the baby. We could have left it all in the past.'

'She hasn't seen you for over thirty years. I don't suppose she'd thought any of it through any more than you had. I think Devon took her by surprise.'

'What do you mean?'

'Come on, Freddie. It must have surprised you how easy it was for all those feelings to come back. It's not going to be any different for her, is it?'

'She's still leaving me though.'

Jo-Jo – August 2015

Amy opened the passenger door and dropped into the seat.

'Is Freddie okay?' I said.

'No,' she said. 'But Jack's with him. What did he say to you, Mum?'

'He told me to leave him alone.'

'Why?'

'I said something stupid and upset him. I told him he needed to get some help, that what he'd done wasn't normal. '

'Sounds pretty spot on to me.'

'I don't know what to do, Amy. I should go back inside and make sure he's okay.'

'I don't think that's a good idea, Mum. Not today.'

'I can't leave it like that.'

'You don't have to. We don't fly until Friday. Let Jack sort him out first.'

A silver Ford Fiesta pulled up in front of us. A nurse in uniform got out of the car and ran up the path of the house opposite. I remembered Jack saying one of his neighbours was expecting her third child. A few spots of rain landed on the front windscreen of the Mazda. I pressed the power button and dabbed the accelerator with my right foot. The engine purred into life. 'You're right,' I said. 'Text Jack and tell him I'll call him tomorrow.'

Freddie – August 2015

Jack's ginger tom cat, Boris, slid around the lounge door and sat on the carpet looking at me. I patted the front of the chair to call him over, but he stood up and walked back out into the hallway, his tail pointing at the ceiling. Jack walked into the lounge carrying two mugs, one full of coffee, which he handed to me, and the other, I could smell, full of liquorice tea. He sat down in the opposite chair.

'You're not still drinking that stuff, are you?' I said.

'It's good for me,' he said, taking a sip and grimacing.

'That must be why you always pull that face when you drink it.'

He took another sip, scrunched up his face again and put the mug down on the glass coffee table. 'You okay?' he said, crossing his legs.

'I'd be better if you stopped asking me that, Jack.'

'You can't expect us all just to forget what you did.'

'I don't expect that, but you're not my counsellor. I just want to get back to normal. I fucked up, but you going all Nurse Ratched on me isn't going to help. You'll be playing Mozart at a low hum next and calling me up for medication time.'

'Fuck off,' he said.

'That's better.'

He uncrossed his legs and sat forward in the chair. 'If you want the truth, I'm pretty pissed off with you. You want to get back to normal. None of us know what that is with you. We're circling you on tiptoes, trying not to say the wrong thing in case you top yourself. No wonder Jo-Jo's leaving. I'm thinking of going with her, but I don't think it'll be far enough way.'

'Don't let me stop you.'

'No point. You'll probably follow me. That's what you do, isn't it? Something dramatic and wait for someone, usually me, to pick up the pieces. Any decisions to be made, and you run and hide. You've never been any fucking different. What did you expect Jo-Jo to do? Fall into your arms and play happy families. She's probably packing right now.'

'I don't need any of you.'

'You need all of us, Freddie. You're useless on your own.'

I stared at the blank television screen, the word useless spooling over and over inside my head. Jo-Jo had said I wasn't normal. No. She'd said what I'd done wasn't normal. She'd looked at me differently, though, like I'd crossed a line, become someone she needed to worry about. She used to say that's what she found attractive, my vulnerability, and even now she kept coming back. I wanted to be different, to be a better man for her, but maybe it was too late, maybe too much time had passed, maybe the train and the tablets were the final fracture. I felt Jack watching me.

'Why did you tell Jo-Jo about the train?' I said.

'I'm not a robot, Freddie. I needed help.'

'But she hates me now.'

'Jesus,' he said. 'You're such a fucking idiot.'

Jo-Jo – January 1980

We'd just watched Eddie Charlton beat Ray Reardon in the *Pot Black* final when Dad made his big announcement. 'We're going to have a birthday tea for your mother tomorrow.'

'No, Joseph,' said Mum from her usual spot on the sofa, smothered in an eiderdown duvet. 'I don't want a fuss.'

'It's all arranged,' said Dad. 'I've asked Arthur to come with his latest.'

'That's a great idea,' said Freddie, who was sat on the opposite chair with me on his lap. 'We'll come.'

I looked at Dad. 'Yeah, of course we will,' I said. 'If that's what Mum wants.'

'I don't feel well enough,' said Mum.

'You'll be fine,' said Dad. 'You don't want to let Arthur down do you?'

Dad's trump card. I always thought Mum had a crush on Arthur, Dad's eldest brother. He used to pick them up in his saloon car and escort Mum arm in arm down the path, opening the back door for her and wiping the seat with his ironed white cotton handkerchief, like she was the Queen Mum. 'For you, my lady,' he'd say. She'd giggle and flush like a sixteen-year-old on her first proper date.

'You shouldn't make a fuss of me, Arthur.'

'I'll make a fuss of who I want. And he'd better treat you right or I'll whisk you away from him.' Dad would smile through pinched lips, as though he wasn't quite getting the joke. When they reached the club, Arthur would run around the car and open the door for Mum to get out. She would always sit there and wait for him.

'No,' said Mum as the *Pot Black* credits rolled up the screen. 'I wouldn't want to let Arthur down.'

*

The next morning, me, Josh and Dad were sitting at the dining table in the kitchen, eating breakfast, when Mum walked in fully dressed. Most mornings Dad had to spend a couple of hours persuading her to get up and, on the days she relented to move downstairs, she'd keep her dressing gown wrapped tight around her body, regardless of the weather, and swap one lying under the duvet place for another by flopping on the settee in the lounge, waiting for Dad to bring her a cup of tea.

'Morning, love,' said Dad when she walked into the kitchen. 'You okay?'

'Of course I'm okay,' she said. 'I'm going to cook some boiled eggs.'

I looked at Josh and we both looked at Dad who stood up, walked over to Mum and tried to guide her towards the lounge. 'I'll do it, love. How many eggs do you want?'

Mum pushed his hand away. 'I'm perfectly capable of boiling some eggs,' she said. 'Now, where did I put that saucepan?' She walked over to the larder cupboard, opened the door, slammed it shut, then the cleaning cupboard, then the fridge. She turned and faced Dad. 'You've hidden them. Why would you do that?'

'Nobody's hidden anything,' he said. 'They're in the cupboard here, where we've always kept them.' He reached into the cupboard next to the sink and pulled out one of the stainless steel saucepans.

Mum ran over and grabbed it out of his hand. 'You're always trying to make me look stupid,' she said.

'Oh, for God's sake, Mum,' I said.

'And you,' she said, glaring at me. 'You're as bad as he is.'

'Calm down, love,' said Dad, putting his hand on her arm.

'I am calm,' screamed Mum.

'Dad's only trying to help,' I said.

'Help. You'd all starve if I wasn't here.'

I laughed. Dad put his other arm around Mum's shoulder. Mum swung around and hit him square in the forehead with the saucepan.

*

Two hours later, me and Josh were sitting on the settee in the lounge, listening to Dad on the phone in the hall.

'That's right, Arthur. She's gone down with a tummy bug. We're going to have to do it another day...'

'Yes. I'm looking after her...'

'Yes. I'll call you tomorrow and let you know how she is...'

'Thank you, Arthur. I'll tell her.'

He hung up the phone and walked into the lounge, still holding his head.

I could see a lump in the middle of his forehead. It was already turning blue. 'You should get that looked at,' I said.

'It's fine,' he said, sitting down in his chair.

'How's Mum?' said Josh.

'She's asleep,' said Dad. 'I managed to get some tablets down her. I don't know what set her off.'

'Apart from being bonkers,' I said.

'You shouldn't say things like that, Jo-Jo.'

'Why not? That's what she is?'

'I'm going out,' said Josh, standing up and walking out of the lounge.

Dad and I flinched as we heard the front door slam behind him.

'What a family,' I said.

'We never used to be like this,' said Dad.

'No...'

'Please don't say it, Jo-Jo. Not now.'

'What? Mention your tart, you mean.'

He held his head in his hands. 'I'm trying my best,' he said.

Jo-Jo – August 2015

The rain started to fall heavily as we drove back to the hotel, the Mazda's automatic windscreen wipers struggling to keep pace with the downpour. Telephone poles and trees whizzed by as the car's wheels hissed through the road puddles. We passed a wind farm, five turbines staggered across a field, their blades rotating at Billy Whizz speed as the breeze geared itself up a few notches. I'd not noticed them before and for a second I wondered if we'd taken a wrong turning. 'Is this the right way?' I said.

'Yes,' said Amy. 'I think so.'

I focussed on watching out for the sharp left turn into the hotel's driveway. I'd sped past it a couple of times on previous journeys and had to do a U-turn.

'We're nowhere near yet,' said Amy, noticing the car slowing down.

'I do know,' I said and then realised I'd snapped. 'I'm sorry. It's this rain. It's making me nervous.'

'He'll be okay with Jack, Mum.'

'I wish I hadn't upset him.'

'You told him the truth.'

'Perhaps he didn't need me to do that today. I'll call him. I don't want to leave it like that.'

'I'm not sure what you're wanting out of this,' said Amy. 'You seem to keep changing your mind. When you came back from Devon you seemed happy, and then you were really sad when he didn't contact you. And now…'

'He's just so frail, Amy. It's like he's two different people. First the train, now the tablets.'

'Neither of them were serious. Jack said he was already stepping back from the edge of the platform when he got to him, and, as for the tablets, he hadn't taken more than some people take as a daily dose. It was all pretty half-hearted.'

'So why do it?'

'To get a reaction off you probably.'

'That's madness.'

'That's what he is, isn't it? A bit bonkers. I spotted that after meeting him once. He thinks you're going to leave him. He told

Jack everyone leaves him in the end, something to do with his Dad dying. But you still love him, don't you?'

I concentrated on the road and thought about Mum. All those years I'd spent telling myself, 'I must try harder. I must try harder.' The rain had slowed down so I pressed my foot on the accelerator. Freddie's face dropped into my head, his broken tooth, his blushing cheeks, his looking down at the floor gaze, his little boy who'd stolen a toffee expression. 'I must try harder.' 'I must try harder.'

'You've missed the turn,' said Amy.

Jo-Jo – November 1974

Me and Dad were in the kitchen, sitting at a pine dining table. In front of us were two bamboo sticks, which Dad had already cut to size and tied together to form an X, and two front pages of the *Daily Mirror* newspaper. One of the pages carried the headline 'Where Did He Go?' and a picture of a moustachioed Lord Lucan who was wanted by the police for the murder of his children's nanny; the other page showed a picture of President Nixon, arms aloft, climbing up the steps of Air Force One with the headline, 'Goodbye America'.

'Watch carefully,' said Dad. 'You might have to do this with your kids one day.'

'I'm watching, Dad,' I said.

He squeezed a line of Golden Gum glue down the side of one of the pages, biting his tongue all the way through to aid his concentration, making sure to get an even spread out of the red rubber spouted lid. Satisfied, he placed the edge of the other page over the line of glue and rubbed his finger all the way along the join, making sure it had stuck firm. Next, he put a blob of glue in each corner of the now joined together pages and glued the X shaped bamboo sticks in place. He picked up a pair of scissors, punctured two pinprick holes through the centre of the newspaper and then threaded through the start of a ball of string, which he tied to the centre cross of the bamboo sticks. 'There,' he said, turning the paper over. 'We have a kite.'

'That's great, Dad. Can we go out and fly it?'

'Best let the glue dry first,' he said. 'Let me take your mum a cup of tea and then we'll try it out.'

An hour later, I climbed into the passenger seat of Dad's Volvo. I was wrapped up tight in my Parka coat, scarf and fingerless gloves. I placed the kite on the backseat. 'I don't know why Josh didn't want to come,' said Dad. 'It's a perfect day for kite flying.'

'You know what he's like,' I said. 'I think he's allergic to the outdoors.'

'Takes after his mum,' said Dad.

'And I take after you,' I said.

He smiled, started up the engine, pulled the car away from the kerb and headed towards the Arboretum.

*

The Arboretum in Walsall was our family go to place for bonfire night. Dad would gather us at the side of the lake, me and Josh staring open-mouthed as the rockets spat and flared skywards, exploding over the water, showering anyone too close with falling fragments of ash. We'd munch on our steaming jacket potatoes bought from the chuckling stallholder, Cyril, who Dad vaguely knew from the Saddlers pub, but who treated us like he was our closest relative – 'Got them kids out again, Joseph. You're lucky. I can't get mine from in front of the telly.'

Mum would glare at Cyril like he was something she wanted to scrape off her shoe. 'Who is that awful man, Joseph?'

'Just some bloke from the pub, love.' We used to cheer when two men doused petrol around the base of the fire stack and dropped lit torches to ignite the whoosh towards a doomed, and slightly dejected looking, Guy Fawkes. I always felt sad, almost tearful, when the flames finally consumed the paper stuffed effigy. Dad would put his arm around me. 'You okay, love?' I'd nod and squeeze him back.

We had our choice of parking bays in the visitors' car park. I retrieved the kite from the backseat and we waded through the piles of autumn shed leaves yet to be swept by the whistling gardeners, the trees shivering in the breeze. At the end of the path, we turned a corner to be greeted by an expanse of undulating field at the back of the lake. I grabbed Dad's hand. The wind notched up its force and made a snatch and grab raid on my breath. I pulled on my faux fur trimmed hood and squeezed Dad's hand tighter. 'Do you think the kite's strong enough, Dad?'

'It'll be fine,' he said. 'Let's go up to the top of that hill.'

We wheezed our way up the steep incline. From the hilltop we could see the whole park yawning to the horizon. 'Isn't it wonderful,' said Dad.

'Perfect,' I said.

'Let's get this baby flying,' he said, holding the kite up in front of him.

The wind started biting at the *Daily Mirror*, trying to wrench it from Dad's grasp. 'Unwind the string a bit,' he said.

I grabbed the ball of string with both hands and walked backwards.

'Ready,' said Dad.

I tightened my grip. 'I'm ready,' I shouted into the wind.

Dad let go of the bamboo sticks and I jolted forwards as the kite pulled on the string, trying to make its escape. Dad grabbed the string as well. 'Roll it out some more,' he shouted.

I took a few more steps backwards, the ball unravelling in front of me. Dad let more of the string pass through his hands, the *Daily Mirror* soaring further and further away. Finally, Dad reached me, there was hardly any string left on the ball. 'Are you strong enough to hold it?' he said.

I nodded and gripped the ball even tighter.

'I'm going to let go after three. One, two…three.'

I was yanked forwards as he released the string. I thought I was going to slip on the dewy grass. I dug my heels in, regained my balance and looked upwards. The kite seemed miles away, on its way to space, backdropped by a thick grey sky and tug, tug, tugging at my arms. 'This is great,' I shouted.

Jo-Jo – August 2015

I pulled the Mazda into its usual parking space in the hotel's car park, pressed the power button to turn off the engine and unfastened my seatbelt. Amy unfastened hers and put up her hand to the hotel security guard, who was waving at us from his usual sentry point by the grey industrial size bins. 'I wonder what he's making of this,' said Amy.

'Yes. I'd wondered that myself.'

'Makes his day a bit more interesting I suppose. He probably goes home and tells his wife about the mad woman and her daughter who've moved into the hotel and their strange goings on.'

'We have been here a long time, Amy. A couple of months now. Is Dan still okay with that?'

'I've told you, Mum, he's booked it at corporate rates for us. He'll sign it off as a tax loss anyway. Stop worrying. You've got enough to think about.'

'I think I'll go and sit in the garden for a bit, clear my head.'

'Well, I'm going to have a soak, try out that new bath bomb I bought. I'll see you at teatime.'

I put my hand on her leg. 'Thank you for coming with me today, sweetheart. I'm afraid your old mum's gone a bit bonkers herself at the moment. Don't give up on me though. I'll work it out.'

'You've always been bonkers,' she said, reaching over and hugging me. 'But it's nice to have a mum who's a bit different.'

We got out of the car. Amy walked off towards the hotel entrance and I walked to the bench underneath the eucalyptus tree and sat down. A red squirrel suddenly ran out from underneath the bushes, stopped in the centre of the lawn, caught my eye for a second before sprinting off, rustling through the long grass in front of the huge oak tree, and emerging to scramble up the trunk and into the sanctuary of the upper branches. I looked up into the tree, but the squirrel was well hidden in the canopy. 'If only it was that simple to escape,' I muttered to myself.

Freddie – February 1980

I walked behind Jo-Jo down the spiral staircase leading from Max's games area to the dance floor, slowing my descent as she carefully placed out the high heels of her yellow Go-Go boots on every step. I could see a gang of lads at the bar, looking up at Jo-Jo and then at me as I turned the corner. Jo-Jo tugged down the hem of her black and white polka-dot Twiggy dress and looked back at me. I smiled and she carried on walking. John Lennon's 'Imagine' started up.

Jo-Jo looked relieved as we reached the bottom of the stairs. She pushed her way through the crowd, heading for the second spiral staircase on the far side of the dance-floor, leading to the restaurant. I started to follow her, but one of the lads from the bar, glazed eyes, blond hair, Tom Selleck moustache, top button open on his white shirt, tie loosened off, stepped out in front of me, his three mates leaning in over his shoulder. 'You jammy bastard,' he shouted in my ear, trying to make himself heard over the music.

I went to walk past him, but he put his hand on my chest. 'How much?' he said.

I looked at him quizzically.

'For the girl. You must be paying her.' He took a sip from his pint of lager and turned back towards his mates. 'Told you she was on the game, lads. I might have a go next week.' They all laughed.

I carried on walking. I could see Jo-Jo waiting for me. I stopped walking, my head was pounding, stuffed with blood. I turned around and walked back towards the bar, my fists squeezed together, my heart racing. One of Tom Selleck's mates saw me and nudged Tom. I squeezed my fists tighter. I felt someone grab my arm. I spun around. 'Freddie,' said Jack.

'Jesus, Jack. I nearly punched you.'

'I could see you were going to punch someone.'

I looked towards the bar. Tom was grinning at me, chewing on the rim of his beer glass, two of his mates had their arms around his shoulders. 'He asked me how much I was paying Jo-Jo.'

'Him. He's a prick.'

'I'm still going to kick his head in.'

He laughed. 'How long have I known you?' he said.

'All my life.'

'And when did you last have a fight?'

I looked at Tom again. Lennon asked everyone to imagine all the people living life in peace. I laughed. Jack put his arm around me. 'Let's face it, Freddie, you're more a lover than a fighter.' He turned me back towards the restaurant and we started walking. We reached Jo-Jo, who was standing at the top of the second staircase. 'Everything okay?' she said.

'Yeah,' I said. 'It's just...'

'Blame me,' said Jack. 'I thought we knew that bloke at the bar.'

'Right,' said Jo-Jo. 'Can we eat now?'

'I'm starving,' I said, grabbing Jo-Jo's hand.

Freddie – September 1973

85

Third day at senior school, me and Jack were leaning against the gym wall, staring at the grey industrial rubbish bin being rocked from side-to-side by four laughing fifth formers, a group of eight or nine older boys standing next to them, clapping, cheering, chanting: 'Rock, rock, rock. Rock, rock, rock,' – the screams from inside the bin echoing off the classrooms and offices of the Victorian courtyard. A bin rocker pointed at me and ran a finger across his throat. 'You're next,' he shouted. Jack and I dropped our eyes.

At that moment, Barrett-Simpson, science teacher, pin-striped suit, straight back, protruding chest, no neck, strode across the courtyard ringing the end of break-time bell. Rumour had him enjoying the corporal punishment a bit too much, slipper for the boys, spanking hand for the girls. 'Get back to your class,' he screamed.

'Thank God,' I said.

'There's always tomorrow,' said Jack. 'We might as well get it over with.'

The fifth-formers walked away, pulling on their too small blazers, patting each other on the back and laughing. The bin rocked gently to a stand-still and an ashen faced, tear-stained eleven-year-old, who looked like he needed a mum, any mum, climbed out. 'You okay,' I shouted. He nodded and ran his arm across his face, snot smearing his cheek. 'You been done yet?' We shook our heads. 'It's fucking terrifying,' he said.

Back in the classroom, 1H chalked on the blackboard, Mr Bloor, our form teacher, bottle-topped spectacles, tracksuit, trainers, standing at the front of the class – 'Get used to me,' he said. 'We've got each other for five years. No slackers. I want us to be the best.'

'Jesus,' I whispered. 'You're going to have to help me get through this, Jack.'

'We'll survive,' he said.

I looked at Mr Bloor again, who'd just thrown a piece of chalk at one of the boys at the back of the class. Five years. I couldn't imaging surviving the rest of the day in this hell hole. Jack squeezed my arm and grinned at me.

Freddie – August 2015

I was in Jack's garden, sitting on the park bench that he'd bought from the local charity shop. I'd gone with him to collect it and twisted my back as we were loading it into his dad's Ford Focus. 'Jesus, Jack. What's this thing made of?'

'It's bomb-proof, mate. It'll outlive me and you.' I looked around the garden and started counting how many different sorts of conifer he'd planted over the last ten years. I'd reached twelve, including the one that crept across the ground, which he'd proclaimed to be rare when he saw it in the garden centre, when the patio door opened and Jack emerged with Bob closely behind him. They each grabbed one of the folded-up wooden patio chairs. Bob smiled at me as he walked across the lawn, Jack kept his eyes on the ground. They reached me, unfolded the chairs and sat down. 'How's it going Freddie?' said Bob, dropping his red Panama hat on the grass.

I looked at Jack. 'I suppose you've told him about Jo-Jo.'

'He's told me,' said Bob. 'The question is, what are you going to do next? We're on your side here, Freddie.'

'There's nothing I can do.'

'You could stop feeling sorry for yourself,' said Jack.

'She's going, Jack. I think I've finally killed it off.'

'Look,' said Bob. 'If you want my opinion as someone who's sort of on the outside…'

It took me a second to realise he was waiting for an answer. 'Which I do,' I said.

'Okay. What you did was stupid.'

I shifted a little on the bench.

'It was, Freddie. There's no point beating about the bush. I know you were upset about the baby, but what you did...'

'You don't have to say it again,' I said.

'The point is,' said Bob, 'Jo-Jo came to see you already knowing what you'd done...'

'She felt sorry for me. That's all. It's what she does. Makes sure everyone's okay.'

'Maybe. But she's going to call you tomorrow. She doesn't have to do that.'

'Amy sent a text,' said Jack.

'She keeps coming back, Freddie,' said Bob. 'Despite you making it really easy for her to walk away, she keeps coming back. Don't you think it's worth one last shot?'

'Maybe it's all best left where it belongs,' I said. 'I keep getting it wrong.'

'So stop doing that,' said Jack, leaning forward in his chair. 'She threw you a curve ball with the baby, but you know that now. Meet her, be honest with her, tell her how you feel.'

'You've got nothing to lose, Freddie,' said Bob.

'I'm not sure,' I said. 'I don't think I'm up to it.'

'Bloody hell,' said Jack.

I started to cry.

Jack dropped off the chair, knelt in front of me and hugged me. 'It's okay,' he said. 'You don't have to do anything you don't want to do.'

'I want to, Jack, but it tears me apart when it goes wrong. I don't think I'm strong enough. Not now.'

Jo-Jo – August 2015

Amy and I were in the hotel conservatory, sitting in our favourite spot next to the yellow daisy patterned jardinière, home for a well-established citrus tree, waiting for our gin and tonics that had become our pre-evening meal ritual. We were alone apart from the Captain Birdseye lookalike and his foot shorter wife, the couple Amy had said looked like a ventriloquist and his dummy on a works outing. 'They've been here as long as we have,' I said.

'I wonder what their story is,' said Amy.

'It can't be any more colourful than the one we're living.'

The waitress walked over, carrying a tray. 'Two gin and tonics, madam?'

Amy nodded and she put the two glasses on the wicker table, handing Amy a slip of paper and a pen. 'You did ask for the Copperhead gin, madam?'

'That's right,' said Amy, signing the paper and handing it back.

The waitress walked away and I lifted up the glass and took a sip. 'I know this gin's expensive,' I said, twirling the ice and lemon around, 'but it is gorgeous.'

Amy picked up her glass and clinked it against mine. 'We deserve it,' she said. 'After the day we've had.' She took a sip of the G&T and leaned back in her chair. 'What are you going to do, Mum?'

'I don't know. It's all such a mess.'

'It needn't be.'

'I know, but, well, we're not exactly straightforward, are we?'

She took another sip of her gin. I took another sip of mine.

'I'll call tomorrow,' I said. 'Make sure he's okay.'

'I wonder what it would have been like,' she said. 'If you and him had stayed together. If he'd waited for you, phoned you. Do you think it would have worked out?'

'Who knows? We were young. We failed the first test, me going off to university, so we couldn't have been that special.'

'Maybe that's the problem,' said Amy. 'The fact that it ended before it began. It's a bit like those film stars who die young – they become legends. And Princess Diana. Who knows what she'd have turned out like, but we all worship her now.'

'You're comparing me and Freddie with Princess Diana.'

'You know what I mean. Maybe you've romanticised it, turned it into something it never really was.'

'If only it were that simple. I feel something caressing me whenever I think about him and a huge chasm opens up inside when I think I'm not going to see him again. It's always been the same.'

'I envy you. I've never felt that about anyone.'

'It's a curse,' I said. 'And it makes it so hard to walk away.'

'So you are walking away.'

'You never met your grandad, Amy.'

'That would have been hard. He died before I was born.'

'But I've told you about him, about how he cared for your Gran.'

'What's that got to do with Freddie?'

'Nothing really, except, well…he is fragile.'

'You're worried you'll have to care for him.'

'I feel awful for thinking it, but I saw what it did to your grandad, what it meant for him, and your Uncle Josh had to do it afterwards. I tried, but I never really got it. I stayed away mostly.'

'That's a bit of a leap, Mum. Gran had Schizophrenia. Freddie's just a bit needy.'

'But look at how he reacts to things, what he does. I'm not sure I want that worry or if I can give him what he needs.'

'It all went okay in Devon, didn't it?'

'It's perfect when he's like that, but his head, when he starts overthinking. You're never too sure what he's going to do, what you're going to get.'

'Sounds like you're scared, Mum, but none of us know what the future holds. I guess it comes down to how much you love him.'

'I'm not sure that's enough.'

'And being without him again. You've just said about the emptiness that will leave.'

'I don't know what to do, Amy.'

She put her glass on the table, reached into her bag and fetched out her phone.

'What are you doing?' I said.

'You need to talk to him, tell him what you've just said to me and then see how you feel. You'll always wonder if you don't.'

'I can't do that over the phone. And phoning him tonight's not a good idea after this morning.'

She turned the phone over in her hand. 'Tomorrow then. I'll text Jack to say we're coming back tomorrow to get this sorted once and for all.'

*

Freddie – August 2015

Bob had fetched a box of Kleenex from inside the house and was sitting on the patio chair, waiting to hand me another one. 'I feel like I might have been a bit hard on you,' he said.

'No. You're right. What I did was stupid. I'm cross with myself for crying.'

'At least you're giving me a chance to play nurse,' said Jack, smiling.

'Seriously, Jack, if I ever need a nurse, I hope she's a lot better looking than you.'

I blew my nose. Bob handed me a fresh tissue. Jack's phone pinged.

'It's a text from Amy,' he said, looking at the screen. 'They want to come back tomorrow to try and sort everything. I'll go and see them and explain.'

'I should be the one explaining,' I said.

'You're not really up to it, are you?'

'What will you say to her?'

'I was hoping you might help me with that.'

I searched my head for a response, but white noise bounced back at me – leaving her at the coach station, not phoning, the baby, the train, the tablets, all the years without her. I wanted it to be okay, to switch off my head for the rest of my life, for Jo-Jo to say it was all going to be okay, to tell me what to do. 'I don't know,' I said. 'It depends on what she says to me.'

Boris came meowing out of the bushes, a crow hanging from his mouth.

'Bloody cat,' said Jack. 'He's dug up that bird I buried yesterday.'

*

Freddie – August 1980

Me and Jo-Jo walked in front of Jack and Karen, down Baslow Road, across the green and, after climbing over the padlocked back-entrance gates to T.P. Riley School, up the dirt track slope to the hidden sanctuary of the white pebble dashed walls of the English Language teaching blocks – our regular Sunday evening snogging retreat.

'I'm not going to kiss you,' Karen said to Jack as we approached the building.

Jack shrugged. 'Don't worry,' he said. 'You really don't do it for me.'

'I'm not sure this a good idea,' said Jo-Jo.

'It's the last chance we've got before you go away,' I said.

'He wants ownership papers,' said Karen. 'I'd tell him to piss off if I were you.'

'It's sweet,' said Jack. 'Shows he cares.'

'I love you,' I said to Jo-Jo.

'Oh my God,' said Karen. 'I think I'm going to vomit.'

Jo-Jo looked nervously at Karen and then back at me. 'Does it really mean that much to you?' she said.

I held her hand. 'I want us to declare our commitment to each other before I lose you for three years.'

'You're not going to lose me, Freddie.'

'You know what I mean.'

'We're fine, aren't we?'

Karen went to say something, but Jo-Jo glared at her.

'It just feels like something we should do,' I said. 'Makes us official.'

Jo-Jo looked at Karen and Jack. She turned back to me. I was still holding her hand. 'Why are these two here?' she said.

'To witness me giving you the ring.'

'You've bought a ring?'

I let go of her hand, reached into the pocket of my jeans and pulled out a red velvet ring box.

'Oh,' said Karen. 'You didn't tell me you were getting a ring.'

'Can you afford this?' said Jo-Jo, taking the box from me.

'I've been saving up. Mum helped a bit. She guessed your ring-size when you tried on that ring of hers?'

She opened the lid, fetched the ring out of the box and looked at me. 'It's gorgeous,' she said.

'It's a DEAREST ring,' I said, taking the nine karat gold ring from her, holding it up to the early evening summer sky, and naming each stone across the front of the band. 'Diamond, Emerald, Amethyst, Ruby, Emerald, Sapphire, Tourmaline...DEAREST.'

'Tourmaline?' said Karen.

'They needed a T,' said Jack and they both sniggered.

'It is lovely, Freddie,' said Jo-Jo.

I took her left hand, held it out in front of me and pushed the ring onto the third finger. 'For all eternity,' I said, looking into her eyes. 'I will love you for all eternity.'

They'd been walking for what seemed like hours through the apple, pear and plum tree orchard of the afterlife, Luther leading the way, easing bushes aside with his shepherd's crook and whistling something tuneless. Chardonnay kept her eyes fixed on the floor, trying to avoid treading on the stray bramble branches and thorns. 'How much further?' she said.

'We're here,' he said, stopping and pointing his stick straight ahead.

She walked to his side. They were standing on a wild grass bank, looking down on a lush lawn clearing. In its centre was a eucalyptus tree. 'It's huge,' she said. 'I can't see the top.'

'It's a reunion tree,' said Luther.

'What happens now?'

'We need the dust arrangers. They'll bring him back to you.' He clapped his hands three times and the dirt at the foot of the tree started to swirl around and around and around, faster and faster, making its way up the trunk. Luther clapped again and a prism of white light dropped from the tree's canopy. The soil floated into the beam, moving higher and higher, disappearing into the eucalyptus branches. 'He's here,' said Luther.

Chardonnay followed his gaze and looked towards the top of the light. A face had dropped into the beam, a chipped tooth, a mischievous grin. She burst into tears.

Freddie – August 2015

Jack beeped the Mini's horn as he drove the car away from the kerb.

'I won't be long,' he'd said as I got out of the car.

'I need to get some fresh clothes, Jack, and to make sure the cats are okay.'

'They're fine. I've been popping in every day.'

'I know. I just need to see for myself.'

I closed the front door, walked down the hall into the kitchen and threw my keys on the table. The only sound was the tick, tick, tick of the Seiko wall clock. Jack had washed up the dirty crocks, two ceramic cat dishes, a single mug, cereal bowl and cutlery, and left them on the worksurface next to the sink, probably not sure where I kept them. There was no sign of the Propranolol. I guessed he'd flushed them down the toilet, used the quickest route to get them out of the house. I thought of my secret stash in the attic, safely stored away in the front of the house soffit space, hidden under old jumpers and t-shirts in a battered copper chest.

I sat down on one of the oak dining chairs and put the tin foil wrapped sandwiches on the kitchen table. Jack had handed them to me just as we were leaving the house. 'Tomato,' he'd said. 'And I've put some fresh milk in your fridge.' I unwrapped the foil and smiled. Tomato with lots of salt. It reminded me of Shirley the Greek, a Dolmio Mamma, who used to be my work partner in one of the care homes. She used to charge one of the octogenarian residents, Henry, a couple of pounds to put his hand inside her bra and squeeze her breast. 'Puts a smile on his face,' she'd say. 'What else will he spend his money on?' The only thing Henry would eat was tomato sandwiches.

A memory: Jo-Jo and I are on our way to Blackpool in my Chrysler Avenger, Springsteen's 'The River' is playing on the car's cassette player. Jo-Jo opens the lid on a Tupperware sandwich box. 'Mum made us a snack,' she says. I take my eyes off the M6 for a moment and look at her.

'Your mum, not your dad?'

'Yep. She must like you. Dad supervised, but I think she did most of it.' She fetches out a piece of fruit cake.

'Oh dear,' she says.

'What?' I say, slowing the car down.

'It's a bit overcooked,' she says. I look at the cake and laugh. 'Overcooked. It's cremated.'

'You've got to try it,' she says, holding it towards my mouth. 'I'm not eating that, Jo-Jo.' She pulls her face into a pained expression.

'I can't believe you'd disrespect my mother.' She brings the cake closer to my mouth. 'Just try a little bit,' she says. 'Just for me.' The first thing I taste is charcoal, like it's been scrapped off the bottom of a wok. I try to bite it.

'Jesus,' I say. 'I think I've broken my tooth.'

'I know,' says Jo-Jo, laughing and closing the lid on the sandwich box. 'Mum's cake is as hard as the knockers of hell. I've never known anyone try a piece before.'

I pushed away the tomato sandwich and picked up my phone.

Jo-Jo – August 2015

I was back in my hotel room, lying on the bed, clutching a black velvet draw string bag, which was about the size of a soap bag. I untied the string and pulled out two red satin boxes, which I laid side by side on the white duvet. I opened the lid of the first box and touched the gold St Christopher, which was slotted into the black sponge base, its chain neatly folded out of sight. Freddie's mum's face dropped into my head, her beaming smile as we realised what she'd bought us, me telling her it would stay with me always. And here it was. Nearly forty years later. Not for the first time, I wished I'd seen more of her, had her in my life for longer. I smiled at the memory of Freddie's blushed cheeks when he'd realised she'd heard us making love, how he couldn't look at her when she came downstairs to watch the *Poseidon Adventure* on that Christmas Day evening in 1979, how she'd kept tutting at him, but smiling and winking at me when he wasn't looking. I touched the St Christopher again and then opened the lid of the second box.

A memory: I'm on my own walking barefoot across the beach in the Maldives. There is a full moon, the beams on the Indian ocean making it look like the sea has frozen silver. I suddenly realise there is something bobbing all over the surface of the water. Luminescent algae. It looks like the stars have fallen out of the sky. Another memory: I'm walking back on my own from the restaurant when I notice three couples and the manager from the hotel reception crouching down in a small huddle at the top of the beach, all of them looking closely at a metal cage that's nestled in the white sand. I walk over and reach them just as the manager lifts the cage to one side and gently starts to scoop the sand underneath. 'What's happening?' I say.

'Turtles,' says the manager. 'We've been waiting for them to hatch for weeks.' I crouch down as well. There's a movement in the sand. The manager stops scooping. A flipper pokes out, flicking the sand aside, closely followed by a turtle head. The baby turtle frees itself and then there's another one, and another one, and another one, scurrying out of the nest and scuttling down the beach towards the sea. More follow, until there are about sixty baby turtles crawling across the white sand, some of them starting to go the wrong way, but quickly realising and joining the race to the sanctuary of the water. We walk slowly behind them and watch as they morph from clumsy land dwellers to Olympic swimmers, disappearing into the aqua blue tide.

I pulled the DEAREST ring out of the second box and slid it gently onto the third finger of my left hand. 'For all eternity,' I whispered.

My phone rang. Freddie's name came up on the screen.

Photograph by TC

Stephen Anthony Brotherton has worked as a Social Worker for the last thirty-five years but has now taken early retirement to work full-time on writing his stories. The Shots trilogy is semi-autobiographical and based on a first love relationship Stephen had at the end of the 1970s and early 1980s. Finally getting these stories out of his head and down on paper has been a cathartic process and a huge tick on his bucket list.